ECHO'S BONES

WORKS BY SAMUEL BECKETT PUBLISHED BY GROVE PRESS

Collected Poems in English and French

The Collected Poems of Samuel Beckett

The Collected Shorter Plays
(All That Fall, Act Without Words I,
Act Without Words II, Krapp's Last Tape,
Rough for Theatre I, Rough for Theatre II,
Embers, Rough for Radio I, Rough for Radio
II, Words and Music, Cascando,
Play, Film, The Old Tune, Come and Go,
Eh Joe, Breath, Not I, That Time, Footfalls,
Ghost Trio, . . . but the clouds . . . , A Piece
of Monologue, Rockaby, Ohio Impromptu,
Quad, Catastrophe, Nacht and Träume,
What Where)

The Complete Short Prose: 1929–1989
(Assumption, Sedendo et Quiescendo,
Text, A Case in a Thousand, First Love, The
Expelled, The Calmative, The End, Texts for
Nothing 1–13, From an Abandoned Work,
The Image, All Strange Away, Imagination
Dead Imagine, Enough, Ping, Lessness,
The Lost Ones, Fizzles 1–8, Heard in the
Dark 1, Heard in the Dark 2, One Evening,
As the story was told, The Cliff, neither,
Stirrings Still, Variations on a "Still" Point,
Faux Départs, The Capital of the Ruins)

Disjecta: Miscellaneous Writings and
a Dramatic Fragment

Echo's Bones

Endgame and Act Without Words

Ends and Odds

First Love and Other Shorts

Happy Days

How It Is

I Can't Go On, I'll Go On:
A Samuel Beckett Reader

Krapps Last Tape:
(All that Fall, Embers, Act Without Words I,
Act Without Words II)

Mercier and Camier

Molloy

More Pricks than Kicks
(Dante and the Lobster, Fingal, Ding-Dong,
A Wet Night, Love and Lethe, Walking Out,
What a Misfortune, The Smeraldina's Billet
Doux, Yellow, Draff)

Murphy

Nohow On
(Company, Ill Seen Ill Said, Worstward Ho)

The Poems, Short Fiction, and Criticism of
Samuel Beckett

Rockaby and Other Short Plays
(Rockaby, Ohio impromptu, All Strange
Away, and A Piece of Monologue)

The Selected Works of Samuel Beckett
(boxed paperback set)
Volume I: Novels
(Murphy, Watt, Mercier and Camier)
Volume II: Novels
(Molloy, Malone Dies, The Unnamable,
How It Is)
Volume III: Dramatic Works
Volume IV: Poems, Short Fiction, Criticism

Stories and Texts for Nothing
(The Expelled, the Calmative, The End,
Texts for Nothing 1–13)

Three Novels
(Malloy, Malone Dies, The Unnamable)

Waiting for Godot

Waiting for Godot: A Bilingual Edition

Watt

Samuel Beckett

ECHO'S BONES

Edited by Mark Nixon

Grove Press

New York

First published in Great Britain in 2014 by
Faber & Faber Ltd

Printed in the United States of America

ISBN 978-0-8021-2045-8
eISBN 978-0-8021-9407-7

Grove Press
an imprint of Grove/ Atlantic, Inc.
154 West 14th Street
New York, NY 10011

Distributed by Publishers Group West

www.groveatlantic.com

14 15 16 17   10 9 8 7 6 5 4 3 2 1

CONTENTS

ACKNOWLEDGEMENTS

My first debt of gratitude is to Edward Beckett, who has supported this publication since its inception several years ago. I would also like to thank the Beckett International Foundation, as well as Special Collections at the University of Reading, the Rauner Library at Dartmouth College in Hanover, the Harry Ransom Humanities Research Center of the University of Texas at Austin and Random House for giving relevant permissions. I have benefited from the help and expertise of a number of scholars in annotating 'Echo's Bones'. Unfortunately, I am unable to pay proper and specific credit to any individual scholar to whom I am indebted for information, as this would have made the entries unwieldy, but wish to acknowledge my debt here. My greatest debt (not for the first, and undoubtedly not for the last time) is to John Pilling, who has grappled with this story for more years than I have, and has generously given me advice, hints and material along the way. He has helped me to clarify various difficult issues, and his annotated edition of Beckett's *Dream* Notebook – the main source for material found in 'Echo's Bones' – has made my task of annotating the text considerably easier. Further sources have been suggested or identified by Chris Ackerley, Aura Beckhöfer-Fialho, Tatyana Hramova, Dirk Van Hulle, Seán Kennedy, Marty Korwin-Pawlowski, the late Seán Lawlor, Paola Nasti, Matthew Scott and David Tucker, and I am grateful to all of them for their help in unravelling several riddles in the text. Thanks are also due to Jim Knowlson for his friendship and support. I am particularly grateful to Dirk Van Hulle, John Pilling and David Tucker for making invaluable comments on reading parts of the manuscript. Needless to say, any omissions and errors that remain are my own, and, given the nature of 'Echo's Bones', I am sure there are quite a few of them. I also want to express my gratitude to Aura for her continued support and to Tikka for the welcome distractions. Finally, I would like to thank the copy-editor, Eleanor Rees, for her careful reading of the manuscript, and Martha Sprackland, Paul Keegan and Matthew Hollis at Faber & Faber for their excellent editorial guidance, their work on the manuscript, and for patiently steering this book into publication.

—*Mark Nixon*

INTRODUCTION

On 25 September 1933, the London publishing house Chatto & Windus accepted Beckett's collection of short stories, *More Pricks Than Kicks*, for publication. Writing to Beckett, Chatto's editor Charles Prentice wondered whether Beckett could add another story, which would 'help the book' by bulking up the content. Beckett agreed, and proceeded to write what he called a 'recessional story' entitled 'Echo's Bones', which was to conclude the collection. Within three days of receiving the story, however, Prentice on 13 November 1933 turned it down, arguing that the story was a 'nightmare' and 'would depress the sales very considerably'. *More Pricks Than Kicks* was published on 24 May 1934 as Beckett had originally submitted it, with ten rather than eleven stories. Now, eighty years after it was first written, the enigmatic 'Echo's Bones' makes its first public appearance.

The failure of 'Echo's Bones' to see the light of day in 1934 needs to be considered in the context of the young writer's desperate struggle to get published in the early 1930s. In many respects, the story of 'Echo's Bones' begins with Beckett's first substantial piece of fiction, the novel *Dream of Fair to Middling Women*, written between May 1931 and July 1932. Encouraged by Chatto's publication of his book on Marcel Proust (*Proust*, 1931), Beckett submitted the novel to the publishers. On receiving it in the summer of 1932, however, Prentice politely called it 'a strange thing', praised those sections in which the writing was 'right away from Joyce', and then unsurprisingly rejected it (5 July 1932). As Prentice told the writer Richard Aldington, turning down Beckett's first novel was 'Perhaps a mistake; but it would have been an almost impossible thing to handle; we didn't understand half of it ourselves' (5 September 1932).

Over the next nine months, the book continued to confuse and alienate publishers. With rejection notices piling up around him, and with no steady income after resigning his lectureship at Trinity College Dublin, Beckett by the middle of 1933 must have realised that *Dream* was never going to be published (it only appeared posthumously in 1992), and subsequently turned his attention to assembling a set of short stories, some of which he had written as early as 1931.

With *Dream* unpublished, and with not enough stories to make up a solid collection that would interest a publisher (or 'invite a publisher to wipe his arse with', in his words), Beckett began to recycle material from the novel, salvaging those sections that could easily be integrated into or adapted to the shorter literary form. Thus for example the story 'A Wet Night', as it appears in *More Pricks Than Kicks*, is taken nearly verbatim from the novel *Dream of Fair to Middling Women*. Beckett also pilfered material from his *Dream* notebook, reading notes collated for the writing of the novel. This pragmatic approach also had, to Beckett's mind, intellectual precedence. He had advocated in his essay on Proust 'that most necessary, wholesome and monotonous plagiarism – the plagiarism of oneself' (523).

By September 1933, Beckett had assembled ten stories amounting to roughly sixty thousand words. After his failure to place his writing with publishers, Beckett was hardly confident that his collection would find favour, despite telling his friend Thomas MacGreevy in a letter of 7 September 1933, and referring to the first story of *More Pricks Than Kicks*, that 'if people can read Saki they can read anything, even Dante & Lobster' (quoted in Pilling 1997, 99). Prentice must have agreed with this evaluation. In his letter of acceptance dated 25 September 1933, he asked whether Beckett could come up with a 'livelier title' to replace 'Draff' (the name of the final story of *More Pricks Than Kicks*), adding 'Hurray too if you manage that extra story', which suggests that Beckett may have raised the issue of writing a further story should the publisher feel that the collection was on the short side. Thanking Beckett for the revised title, *More Pricks Than Kicks*, Prentice reiterated his belief that 'another 10,000 words, or even 5,000 for that matter, would, I am certain, help the book' (29 September 1933). Beckett, for various reasons, struggled to accommodate the request. As he told MacGreevy, part of the problem was that he had killed off the protagonist of the collection in the penultimate story, 'Yellow': 'I have to do another story for More Pricks, Belacqua redivivus, and I'm as stupid as a goat' (9 October 1933; *Letters of Samuel Beckett I* 167). The fact that Belacqua would have to be resurrected for the new final story was acknowledged by Prentice: 'I'm delighted that Belacqua Lazarus will be walking again shortly' (4 October 1933). By early November, Beckett confessed to MacGreevy that he was 'grinding out the last yelps for C. & W.' but was 'having awful trouble' with it (1 November 1933). Yet he must have succeeded in writing the story rather quickly after this, as Prentice acknowledged receipt of it on 10 November, while also registering his surprise at its length of 13,500 words ('What a big one!'). More importantly, the story as a whole completely confounded him, and in a long letter, phrased apologetically yet firmly, Prentice informed Beckett on 13 November that 'Echo's Bones' was not suitable for publication; the letter is worth citing at length:

> *It is a nightmare. Just too terribly persuasive. It gives me the jim-jams. The same horrible and immediate switches of the focus, and the same wild unfathomable energy of the population. There are chunks I don't connect with. I am so sorry to feel like this. Perhaps it is only over the details, and I may have a correct inkling of the main impression. I am sorry, for I hate to be dense, but I hope I am not altogether insensitive. 'Echo's Bones' certainly did land on me with a wallop.*
>
> *Do you mind if we leave it out of the book – that is, publish 'More Pricks than Kicks' in the original form in which you sent it in? Though it's on the short side, we'll still be able to price it at 7/6d. 'Echo's Bones' would, I am sure, lose the book a great many readers. People will shudder and be puzzled and confused; and they won't be keen on analysing the shudder. I am certain that 'Echo's Bones' would depress the sales very considerably.*
>
> *I hate having to say this, as well as falling behind scratch myself, and I hope you will forgive as far as you can. Please try to make allowances for us; the future of the book affects you as well.*
>
> *This is a dreadful débâcle – on my part, not on yours, God save the mark. But I have to own up to it. A failure, a blind-spot, call it what I may. Yet the only plea for mercy I can make is that the icy touch of those revenant fingers was too much for me. I am sitting on the ground, and ashes are on my head.*

Beckett's response to this remarkable letter appears to have been tempered by acquiescence, although a possibly more honest reaction is found in a letter to MacGreevy written shortly

afterward: 'I haven't been doing anything. Charles's fouting
à la porte [kicking out] of Echo's Bones, the last story, into
which I put all I knew and plenty that I was better still aware of,
discouraged me profoundly [. . .]. But no doubt he was right. I
tell him so, therefore all that entre nous' (6 December 1933; *Letters of Samuel Beckett I* 171). Indeed, the failure of the story provoked Beckett into writing a poem of the same name, and he
subsequently used the title again for his first collection of poems, *Echo's Bones and Other Precipitates* (1935). And, although
it would surely have been difficult for him to feel otherwise at
the time, the writing of the story was not an entirely wasted effort, as he transferred material from 'Echo's Bones' to a revised
ending of 'Draff', and thus to *More Pricks Than Kicks* as a whole;
Prentice (on 11 December 1933) praised 'the new little bit at the
end', calling it 'a decided improvement.'

On first reading 'Echo's Bones', one cannot help but sympathise with Prentice's decision to reject the story. As an early
critic, Rubin Rabinovitz, summarised it: 'the setting is unrealistic, the plot improbable, the characters bizarre' (55). 'Echo's
Bones' is a difficult, at times obscure story, uneven in tone
and mood, and evasive in stating its business. It bristles with
tensions that arise from its fragmented nature, its incessant
intertextual borrowings, the way it shifts between different
literary styles and its allusive, wayward language, none of
which allow the story to coalesce into a unity, even of the
'involuntary' kind that characterised *Dream of Fair to Middling Women*. But if the story is rather wild and undisciplined, it is also quite brilliantly so, especially in the flaunting
yet withholding of its 'shabby mysteries' ('Draff', 183). The

imaginative playfulness mixes styles and sources, all of which gesture towards Joyce but ultimately establish something rather more distinctly Beckettian.

Beckett obviously struggled to write the story. His correspondence with MacGreevy testifies to the fact that his heart was not really in the book as a whole ('But it is all jigsaw and I am not interested'), viewing *More Pricks Than Kicks* as a concession to the marketplace, and in terms of literary merit inferior to what he had tried to do with the novel *Dream*. Moreover, Beckett's feelings about his creative activities must have been complicated by the death of his father only a few months earlier (on 26 June 1933), which may have contributed to his decision to abandon the kind of allusive, fragmentary and ultimately Joycean writing that might fulfil his own artistic criteria but would not sustain a living. As a result, Beckett's struggle to write the story is evident across the surface of the text. The characters themselves are ostensibly trying to keep a story going even as it tries at every turn to sabotage them from doing so. More than once, for example, the text obstructs itself, as when Lord Gall 'could not go on with what he was saying.'

Naturally enough, the largest challenge facing Beckett in writing this 'fagpiece', as the story calls itself, was how to ensure its consistency within the collection as a whole. He must have decided that it was easier to resurrect Belacqua from the dead and to add a story at the end of the book than to upset the unity, if there is one, of *More Pricks Than Kicks* by inserting one at an earlier point. Throughout the volume, Belacqua negotiates a world of love and death, and in 'Echo's Bones' is faced with an afterlife. Even before his untimely demise during a surgical operation in the story 'Yellow', Belacqua was described (in *Dream*) as a 'horrible border-creature' (123), a state of being reinforced in 'Echo's Bones' by his opening position, seated on a fence. Although a ghost, and casting no shadow, Belacqua is very much a corporeal entity, brought back to life in order to atone for his narcissism, his solipsism and for being an 'indolent bourgeois poltroon' (174) in the previous stories, indolent like his namesake in Dante's *Divine Comedy*.

The story self-referentially calls itself a 'triptych', and it is indeed a piece in three movements, but whose panels barely make up a whole. The first part tells the story of Belacqua's resurrection and his encounter with the prostitute Miss Zaborovna Privet. The second deals with the giant Lord Gall of Wormwood, who is unable to father a son and will lose his estate to the fertile Baron Extravas should he die intestate. Lord Gall thus requests that Belacqua help make him a father; Belacqua complies, and Lady Moll Gall does indeed give birth – to a girl, since this is a shaggy dog story. The story then switches in its final part abruptly to Belacqua sitting on his own headstone, watching the groundsman Doyle rob his grave. Although Doyle had already appeared as an unnamed minor figure in 'Draff', the other main characters are new to the collection. But in an attempt to establish a sense of continuity between 'Echo's Bones' and the other stories of *More Pricks*, Beckett reintroduces various characters despite having killed off several of them (including Belacqua) in the course of the book, as summarised during the opening of 'Draff': 'Then shortly after that they suddenly seemed to be all dead, Lucy of course long since, Ruby duly, Winnie to decency, Alba Perdue in the natural course of being seen home' (175). Nevertheless, at two points in 'Echo's Bones' a parade of characters passes by in the background. Thus for example the Parabimbis and Caleken Frica make an appearance, as does the (deceased) Alba, one of Belacqua's love interests, who surfaces surreally in a submarine transporting the souls of the dead. The reintroduction of these characters, who add nothing to the plot, or plots, presumably prompted Prentice's reference to the 'wild unfathomable energy of the population'.

As for the 'horrible and immediate switches of focus', there is hardly a sentence in 'Echo's Bones' that is not borrowed from one source or another, bearing out Beckett's own statement that he had 'put all I knew and plenty that I was better still aware of' into the story. These references range from the recondite to the popular (Marlene Dietrich, French chansons), and are inscribed in the text both openly and covertly. In compositional terms, 'Echo's Bones' mainly draws on the so-called *Dream* Notebook; essentially Beckett used those quotations from this artistic notebook that he had not previously used in the novel of the same name or in *More Pricks Than Kicks*. Either Beckett was grasping around for whatever he had to hand, in his haste to complete this last story for Chatto & Windus, or he was re-enacting a compositional strategy that had been impressed upon the young writer by Joyce's example. 'Echo's Bones' is, without doubt, more densely allusive, more Joycean, than any of Beckett's other early writings; both on a verbal and a structural level, it harnesses a range of materials, from science and philosophy to religion and literature. As its title suggests, this is a story made up of echoes, of allusions to multiple cultural contexts. However, as John Pilling has remarked, at times there are so 'many echoes that they seem to multiply to infinity, and yet they are little more than the bare bones of material without any overarching purpose to animate' (Pilling 2011, 104). The switches between the three parts of the story, as well as the references, both erudite and contemporary, seem randomised, all of which is compounded by the shifts in register. The style draws on various literary periods, and the language oscillates between the ornate ('Archipelagoes of pollards, spangled with glades') and the demotic (Dublin slang).

The story structurally and conceptually parallels Dante's glimpse of the afterlife in the *Divine Comedy*, and plays on forms of atonement that correspond to the sinner's actual vices. The pervasively purgatorial tone is compounded by phrases taken from the Bible, as well as from Thomas à Kempis's *The Imitation of Christ* and Jeremy Taylor's *The Rule and Exercises of Holy Living and Holy Dying* (1650-1), the latter a book Beckett was reading at the time he was composing the story. However, and despite the many quotations from St Augustine's *Confessions*, this is not a story of punishment, conversion and salvation. Indeed, any possibility of religious salvation for Belacqua is undercut by the litter of sexual puns (learned or schoolboy), lewd jokes, and terminology deriving from flagellation, infertility and homosexuality, especially in the second part of the story. The themes of impotence and sterility are woven through the story, clothed in literary as well as sexual allusions. The threat of reproductive sex, visible across Beckett's early work, is here deflected humorously, and the general profanity owes much to the Marquis de Sade, whose *120 Days of Sodom* Beckett was later to consider translating into English.

The struggle to identify what is at stake in the story is made more difficult by the employment of devices from fantastical, non-realist genres and narratives. One such area is myth; as the title already suggests, Beckett employs the story of Narcissus and Echo from Ovid's *Metamorphoses* to frame Belacqua's 'post-obit' journey from living character to echoic voice, until only his bones remain in the final tableau of the story. Beckett also invests the proceedings with a gothic atmosphere, especially in the final section, which plays out in a cemetery. Perhaps more surprising is the use of fairy tale, a form which throws longer shadows over Beckett's early oeuvre than is usually acknowledged. Blending fairy tales, gothic dreams and classical myth, 'Echo's Bones' is in parts a fantastical story replete with giants, tree-houses, mandrakes, ostriches and mushrooms, drawing on a tradition of folklore as popularised by W. B. Yeats and the Brothers Grimm, for example.

Beckett's experiments with the fairy tale form, and the general hilarity of the knock-about between Belacqua and Lord Gall, obscure but never quite obliterate the sense of grief and absence that pervades the story. Indeed, as its opening words indicate, 'the dead die hard', and Beckett may well have had the death of his cousin and lover, Peggy Sinclair (in May 1933, of tuberculosis), and that of his father (in June 1933), on his mind when writing the story. Indeed, the various clusters of motifs – resurrection, graveyards, legal issues of estates and successions, and the fact that Lord Gall has no son, just as Beckett has no father – suggest a preoccupation too distressing to be stated more directly. Whereas in the literary world of *Dream of Fair to Middling Women* it was 'remarkable how everything can be made to end like a fairy tale', in the real world this was simply not possible. As such the final words of 'Echo's Bones' (which occur twice in the story), taken from the Brothers Grimm, fuse the fairy-tale element with a tone of resignation and acceptance: 'So it goes in the world'. As 'Echo's Bones' is a story about absent fathers and sons, about the afterlife and about the deplorable state of the world, it is hardly surprising that its main literary dialogue is with Shakespeare's *Hamlet*. On both a thematic and a verbal level, *Hamlet* ghosts through 'Echo's Bones'.

It is of course impossible to ascertain whether early readers would have 'shuddered' with confusion, as Prentice predicted, when reading 'Echo's Bones' as part of *More Pricks Than Kicks*; or, put differently, whether the story actually 'belongs' to that collection. One could argue that Beckett, in the knowledge that he had a contract for the stories, went back to the way of writing he preferred at the time, the exuberant yet enigmatic style of *Dream of Fair to Middling Women*. In any case, while it is interesting to read 'Echo's Bones' as part of the collection it was intended to conclude, it stands on its own. And we need see it neither as a step toward Beckett's farewell to Joyce's accumulative style of writing, by clearing out his store of quotations, nor as an emotionally charged text which – as Walter Draffin's book is described in the *More Pricks* story 'What a Misfortune' – was simply 'a mere dump for whatever he could not get off his chest in the ordinary way' (133). The literary merit of 'Echo's Bones' is evident; moreover, it is a vital document, which represents the missing link in Beckett's development during the 1930s, and suggestively anticipates the postwar texts, stating a conundrum which will be restated in *Waiting for Godot* and beyond: 'They give birth astride of a grave, the light gleams an instant, then it's night once more.' 'Echo's Bones' allows us to witness a young writer at ease yet at odds with the cultural contexts of his time, attempting to forge a literary path.

NOTE ON THE TEXT

Samuel Beckett's story 'Echo's Bones' survives in one type-script, held at the Rauner Library at Dartmouth College, and a carbon copy held in the A. J. Leventhal Collection at the Harry Ransom Center at the University of Texas at Austin. The two texts are thus identical, but there are differences in Beckett's manuscript corrections. The Dartmouth typescript (given by Beckett to the critic Laurence Harvey in 1962) has all of the corrections made to the Austin copy, but also has further corrections, and thus forms the base text for this edition. Underlined words have been retained.

Typographical errors that remain in Beckett's typescript have been silently corrected, but more substantive changes are listed below; Beckett's manuscript corrections, if of interest, are discussed in the annotations.

[p. 7]: The word 'the' has been added to the sentence 'But her first impression was confirmed by the absence of any shadow [. . .]'.

[p. 8]: The word 'a' has been added to the sentence 'Now the fact of the matter is that a personal shadow is like happiness [. . .]'.

[p. 9]: In footnotes 1 and 2, Beckett writes 'Cf.' and 'Cp.' respectively; this has been standardised by using 'Cf.' in both instances.

[p. 12]: A third point has been added to the ellipses at the end of the sentence 'Now if there should turn out to be a Voltigeur in this assortment . . . !'. Beckett uses both two- and three-point ellipses before other punctuation in this manner; this has been standardised throughout the text to use three.

[p. 13]: Beckett's spelling of 'exageration' has, in both instances the word occurs, been changed to 'exaggeration'.

[p. 14]: Beckett initially wrote 'mentioned that he was bemired bemired with sins'; it is unlikely, if not impossible, that he intended the repetition, so one occurrence of the word 'bemired' has been omitted.

[p. 20]: In citing Jeremy Taylor's *Holy Dying*, Beckett writes 'Duke of Ebenberg' instead of Duke of Ebersberg; this error has been corrected here.

[p. 32]: The word 'considerable' has been changed to 'considerably'.

[p. 36]: Beckett's reference on this page and on p. 97 to 'page 7, paragraph 2' refers to a passage in his own typescript, rather than this edition.

[p. 41]: The word 'been' has been added to the sentence "'I dassay my life was a derogation and an impùdence" said Belacqua "which it was my duty, nay should have been my pleasure, to nip in the wombbud"'.

[p. 42]: The sentence 'There you glump like a fluke in a tup and what to know from what' has been changed to 'There you glump like a fluke in a tup and want to know from what'.

[p. 47]: The word 'be' has been added to the sentence "'In the event of dispute" said Doyle, "it might be a wise thing to appoint an arbitrator"'.

Sam
Beckett.

ECHO'S BONES

The dead die hard, they are trespassers on the beyond, they must
take the place as they find it, the shafts and manholes back into
the muck, till such time as the lord of the manor incurs through his
long acquiescence a duty of care in respect of them. They they are
free among the dead by all means, then their troubles are over,
their natural troubles. But the debt of nature, that scandalous zx
post-obit on one's own estate, can no more be discharged by the mere
fact of kicking the bucket than descent can be made into the same
stream twice. This is a true saying.

At least it can be truly said of Belacqua who now found himself
up and about in the dust of the world, back at his old games in the
dim spot, on so many different occasions that he sometimes wondered
if his lifeless condition were not all a dream and if on the whole
he had not been a great deal deader before than after his formal departure, so to speak, from among the quick. No one was more willing
than himself to admit that his definite individual existence had in
some curious way been an injustice and that this tedious process of
extinction, its protracted faults of old error, was the atonement
imposed on every upstart into animal spirits, each in the order of
time. But this did not make things any more pleasant or easy to bear.
It occurred to him one day as he sat bent double on a fence like a
casse-poitrine in delicious rêverie and puffed away at his Romeo and
Juliet that perhaps if he had been cremated rather than inhumed directly he would have been less liable to revisit the vomit. But happily for all of us this thought was too egregious to detain him long.
He tried all he knew, without shifting his position however, to conceive of his exuviae as preserved in an urn or other receptacle in
some kind person's sanctum or as drifting about like a cloud of
randy pollen, but somehow he could not quite bring it off, this simple little flight. Was it possible that his imagination had perished
in the torture chamber, that non-smoking compartment? That would
indeed be something to be going on with, that would be what a Madden
prizeman, his eyes out on stalks like a sentinel-crab's with zeal
and excitement, would call a step in the right direction.

To state it then fairly fully once and for all, Belacqua is a
human, dead and buried, restored to the jungle, yes really restored
to the jungle, completely exhausted, conscious of his shortcomings,
sitting on this fence, day in day out, having this palpitation,
picking his nose between cigars, suffering greatly from exposure.
This is he and the position from which he ventures, to which he is
even liable to return after the fiasco, in which he is installed for
each dose of expiation of great strength, from which he is caught
up each time a trifle better, dryer, less of a natural snob. These
predicates do not cover him, no number of them could. If as dense
tissue of corporeal hereditaments - ha! - he was predicateless, how
much more so then as spook? But cover they do the mean, the least
presentable, aspect of his cruel reversion, three scenes from which,

ECHO'S BONES

The dead die hard, they are trespassers on the beyond, they must take the place as they find it, the shafts and manholes back into the muck, till such time as the lord of the manor incurs through his long acquiescence a duty of care in respect of them. Then they are free among the dead by all means, then their troubles are over, their natural troubles. But the debt of nature, that scandalous post-obit on one's own estate, can no more be discharged by the mere fact of kicking the bucket than descent can be made into the same stream twice. This is a true saying.

At least it can be truly said of Belacqua who now found himself up and about in the dust of the world, back at his old games in the dim spot, on so many different occasions that he sometimes wondered if his lifeless condition were not all a dream and if on the whole he had not been a great deal deader before than after his formal departure, so to speak, from among the quick. No one was more willing than himself to admit that his definite individual existence had in some curious way been an injustice and that this tedious process of extinction, its protracted faults of old error, was the atonement imposed on every upstart into animal spirits, each in the order of time. But this did not make things any more pleasant or easy to bear. It occurred to him one day as he sat bent double on a fence like a casse-poitrine in delicious rêverie and puffed away at his Romeo and Juliet that perhaps if he had been cremated rather than inhumed directly he would have been less liable to revisit the vomit. But happily for all of us this thought was too egregious to detain him long. He tried all he knew, without shifting his position however, to conceive of his exuviae as preserved in an urn or other receptacle in some kind person's sanctum or as drifting about like a cloud of randy pollen, but somehow he could not quite bring it off, this simple little flight. Was it possible that his imagination had perished in the torture chamber, that non-smoking compartment? That would indeed be something to be going on with, that would be what a Madden prizeman, his eyes out on stalks like a sentinel-crab's with zeal and excitement, would call a step in the right direction.

To state it then fairly fully once and for all, Belacqua is a human, dead and buried, restored to the jungle, yes really restored to the jungle, completely exhausted, conscious of his shortcomings, sitting on this fence, day in day out, having this palpitation, picking his nose between cigars, suffering greatly from exposure. This is he and the position from which he ventures, to which he is even liable to return after the fiasco, in which he is installed for each dose of expiation of great strength, from which he is caught up each time a trifle better, dryer, less of a natural snob. These predicates do not cover him, no number of them could. If as dense tissue of corporeal hereditaments – ha! – he was predicateless, how much more so then as spook? But cover they do the mean, the least presentable, aspect of his cruel reversion, three scenes from which, the first, the central and the last, we make bold to solicit as likely material for this fagpiece, this little triptych.

To begin then at the beginning, he felt himself nodding in the grey shoals of angels, his co-departed, that thronged the

womb-tomb, distinctly he felt himself lapsing from a beati-
tude of sloth that was infinitely smoother than oil and softer
than pumpkins, he found himself fighting in vain against the
hideous torpor and the grit and glare of his lids on the eyeballs
so long lapped in gloom, and the next thing was he was horsed
as it were for major discipline on the fence as see above, the
bells pealing in all the steeples, his pockets crammed with
cigars. He took the band off one of these, lit it, looked into his
heart and exclaimed:

'My soul begins to be idly goaded and racked, all the old
pains and aches of me soul-junk return!'

Hardly had this thought burst from his brain as a phos-
phate from the kidneys when a woman shot out of the hedge
and stood before him, serene yet not relaxedly gay. There she
stood, frankly alluring him to come and doubt not, stretching forth to hug him her holy hands pullulant with a million
good examples. There was nothing at all of the grave widow or
anile virgin about her, nothing in the least barren in her appearance. She would be, if she were not already, the fruitful
mother of children of joys.

'They call me Zaborovna' she simpered.

'I don't hear what you say' said Belacqua. 'Speak up will
you.'

Now it must be clearly understood that there were no stews
where Belacqua came from, no stews and no demand for stews.
But here in the dust with night getting ready to fall it was quite
a different matter. Belacqua felt he had been dead a long time,
forty days at least.

'You are Belacqua' she said 'whom we took for dead, or I'm
a Dutchman.'

'I am' said Belacqua, 'restored for a time by a lousy fate to the nuts and balls and sparrows of the low stature of animation. But who is we and who are you?'

'I told you' she said, 'Zaborovna, at your service; and we, why little we is just an impersonal usage, the Tuscan reflexive without more.'

'The mood' said Belacqua, 'forgive the term, of self-abuse, as the English passive of masochism.'

'How long do you expect to be with us?' said Zaborovna.

'As long as I lived' said Belacqua, 'on and off, I have the feeling.'

'You mean with intermissions?' she said.

'Do you know' said Belacqua, 'I like the way you speak very much.'

'The way I speak' she said.

'I find your voice' he said 'something more than a roaring-meg against melancholy, I find it a covered waggon to me that am weary on the way, I do indeed.'

'So musical' she said, 'I would never have thought it.'

It was high time for a pause to ensue and a long one did. The lady advanced a pace towards the fence, clearly she was sparring for an opening, Belacqua pulled furiously at the immense cigar, a bird, its beak set in the heaven, flew by.

'Too late!' he exclaimed at last in piercing tones. 'Too late!'

'What is too late?' said Zaborovna.

'This encounter' said Belacqua. 'Can't you see my life is over?'

'Oh' she said, in a voice something between a caress and a dig in the ribs, 'I wouldn't go so far as to say that.'

In the echo of the above pause she seized her opportunity,

transferred her slyly grave deportment to the knees and thighs of the revenant, which parts of him trembled in the chill of the hour. A colony of rooks made their evening flight and darkened the sky, yes actually darkened the sky. Belacqua polished off his cigar, pressed it out fiercely against the rail, elevated his mind to God, crossed himself a thousand times.

'Forgive me' he said, 'I'm as bad as Dr Keate of Eton, I can see his shaggy red brows distinctly, I can't recall your name for the moment.'

'Zaborovna' she said, 'yours to command, Miss Zaborovna Privet, put your arm about her won't you.'

Belacqua, whom nothing could teach not to spit and dig for clotted mucus in the presence of ladies, shanghaied now a snot on his cuff and brought his eyes that were so sore with one thing and another, whinging and the light that quick-change artist, close up to those, sparklers of the first water and in which he seemed to discern a number of babies, of the Privet, who after a short and gallant struggle was constrained to look away, so searing, so red-hot and parallel, were the prongs of his gaze. Away she looked to the cool, not to say bitter, east and observed her shadow, like an old man's desire, prone and monstrous on the grass, but not a sign of her pick-up's, out of whose lap she sprang at once and stood on the ground well to one side, thinking that perhaps she had been seeing single, and looked again. But her first impression was confirmed by the absence of any shadow but the fence's and her own, projected in tattered umber far across the waste. The sun was there all right, belting away in the west behind, ignoring him completely. This body that did not intercept the light, this packet of entrails that had shed the ashen spancels, she looked

it up and down. He had produced a razor from some abyssal
pocket and was lovingly whittling a live match. This when
pointed according to his God he used to pierce a deep meatus
in a fresh cigar, visit his teeth all round, top and bottom, light
the cigar. Then he made to throw it away but recovered himself
in time and stuck it like a golf tee in the stuff of his pullover.

Tears rushed down the cheeks of Zaborovna as she hurled
herself into the arms of her prey, no easy matter.

'Wipe them' said Belacqua.

He was most ardent and sad all of a sudden, a Gilles de Rais
twinkle in his eye. How long then was this, this – ha! – strangury of decency going to go on, going to go on. The Privet was
present, panting away to no apparent avail, wilful waste, like
the beatific paps of a nun of Minsk; while as for himself, cold
as January at the best of times, he was no more capable now,
when any moment might be the last of the current lot, ring
him back to the gloom where stews and therefore Privets had
no sense, of rising to such a buxom occasion than Alfieri or
Jean-Jacques of dancing a minuet. Yet he was sorely tempted
to try, that was the bitch of it.

'Dry those handsome eyes' he said as distinctly as the cigar
would allow. 'Don't drown the babies I see there for a corpse
in torment.'

He withdrew the cigar, put his features into a sudden spin
of anguish, righted them no less abruptly, replaced the cigar.
That was the kind of thing he meant, that was the torment
coming to the surface to breathe. Now she knew.

Soothed by this kind clonus she said:

'It is not so much you as your shadow. What has befallen it?'

Now the fact of the matter is that a personal shadow is like happiness, possession of being well deceived, hypnosis, (1) apprehensible only as a lack. A stranger's shadow, the shadows of natural things, of trees, wings, ocean clouds and the rest, one goes honing after these and indeed it is hard to imagine how one could ever manage without them. But one's own, except in the case of a very nervous subject, (2) is as unobtrusive as the motion of the earth, to adopt the system of Galileo, that dials it.

Belacqua looked wildly about him.

'God I don't know at all' he exclaimed. 'I thought I had it.'

Zaborovna delivered herself now and not a moment too soon of the butterfly doctrine noted above. It was true, she said, of more things than heartsease (a woman's term) and shadow. It was only a chance, she said, that she had seen hers at all. She would pay more attention to it in future. She looked to make sure it was still there.

'You may be right' said Belacqua. 'I don't say you're not. I'm a marked man whatever way you look at it.'

There is more in it than that, thought Zaborovna, but hist!

'Every evening during the season' she said, 'Saturdays excepted, I lend myself to sublime delinquencies in the old town where I lodge, and lodge in some splendour believe me. Happily to-night I am not booked.'

The sun set, the rooks flew home. Why did Belacqua always seem to be abroad at this hour of lowest vitality surely? Portions of a poem by Uhland came into his mind. They received short shrift.

'No crows where I come from' he said, 'God be praised.'

1. Cf. Titania and the Ass.
2. Cf. Richard III.

'Ah' said Zaborovna. 'Then there is a God after all?'

'Presumably' said Belacqua. 'I know no more than I did.'

He seemed to have recovered from his sense of bereavement. Nevertheless she was right, there was more in it, as the sequel may well show, than he thought.

'I should be happy to put you up' said Zaborovna.

A long black cylindrical Galloway cow, in her heyday a kind and quick feeder, now obviously seriously ill with rinderpest, red-water and contagious abortion, staggered out of the ground fog, collapsed and slipped calf. It was all over in a flash.

'Happy to put you up' said Zaborovna.

'When you say "put me up"' said Belacqua, 'what do you mean exactly?'

Not having properly sized up her man she kept the wrong things back.

'You are far too hospitable' said Belacqua, 'I couldn't dream of it.'

The cow, greatly eased, on her back, her four legs indicting the firmament, was in the article of death. Belacqua knew what that was.

'And you don't utter all your mind' he said, 'unless I am greatly mistaken.'

'Well then' she said, 'fried garlic and Cuban rum, what do you say to that?'

'Human rum!' exclaimed Belacqua.

'Cuban' she said, 'a guinea a bottle.'

Something simply had to happen, the ground-fog lifted, the sky was mare's-tail and shed a livid light, ghastly in the puddles that pitted the land, but beautiful also, like the complexion in Addison's disease. A child, radiant in scarlet diaper and pale blue pilch, skipped down off the road and began to sail a boat.

'Though you hedge' said Belacqua, 'Miss Privet, yet do you win, and my shame be my glory.'

'That's a sensible cadaver' said Zaborovna. She began to back away most gracefully.

'Let the deadbeats get on' said Belacqua, 'I can't bear a crowd.'

The faithful, seeded with demons, a dim rabble, cringing home after Vespers, regrettably not Sicilian. In the van an Editor, of a Monthly masquerading as a Quarterly, his po hat cockaded fore and aft with a title-page and a poem of pleasure, a tailor of John Jameson o'Lantern dancing before him; next, a friend's wife, splendid specimen of exophthalmic goitre, storming along, her nipples up her nose; next, a Gipsy Rondo, glabrous but fecund, by-blow of a long line of aguas and ilu-minaciones; next, Hairy, leaning back, moving very stiff and open; next, in a covered Baby Austen, the Count of Parabimbi and his lady; next, trained to a hair, a nest of rank outsiders, mending in perfect amity a hard place in Eliot, relaxing from time to time to quire their manifesto: 'Boycott Poulter's Meas-ure!'; next, as usual in the thick of the mischief, a caput of highly liberally educated ex-eunuchs, rotating slowly as they tottered forward, their worn buttocks gleaming through the slits in their robes; next, Caleken Frica, stark staring naked, jotting notes for period dialogue with a cauter dipped in cocoa round the riddle of her navel minnehaha minnehaha; next, a honeymoon unicorn, brow-beating his half-hunter; next, a Yogi milkman, singeing his beard with a standard candle, a contortionist leprechaun riding in his brain (abdominal); next, the sisters, Debauch and Death, holding their noses. So

they passed by and passed away, those mentioned and one or
two more, the second after the first, the third after the second,
and so forth in order, until the last – a fully grown androgyne
of tempestuous loveliness – after the rest, and after the last a
spacious nothing.

'Bad one by one' said Belacqua, 'very bad all together.'

A frightful sound as of rent silk put the heart across him.

'There never was such a season for mandrakes' said
Zaborovna.

'Alas' said Belacqua, 'Gnaeni, the pranic bleb, is far from being a mandrake. His leprechaun lets him out about this time
every Sunday. They have no conduction.'

The dead cow would soon be a source of embarrassment.

'You remember the wonderful lines' said Belacqua:

> *A dog, a parrot or an ape . . .*
> *Engross the fancies of the fair.'*

Zaborovna let a ringing guffaw.

'Did you see the Parabimbi' she said. 'Where did she get her
crucified smile, the little immaculate conception?'

Belacqua descended resolutely from the fence, took up a
hole in his belt, plunged his hand into his pocket and pulled
out a Partagas, the sweetest contingency by a long chalk
to come his way for many a day, lit it, thought, Now if there
should turn out to be a Voltigeur in this assortment . . . !, and
said:

'Whenever you are ready Miss.'

She tossed back the hissing vipers of her hair, her entire
body coquetted and writhed like a rope, foamed into a bawdy
akimbo that treed, cigar and all, her interlocutor. Poor fellow,

there he was, petrified, back on the fence. And Zaborovna, one minute the picture of exuberant continence, the next this Gorgon! Truly there is no accounting for some people. Women in particular seem most mutable, houses of infamous possibilities. So at least it seemed to Belacqua, not for the first time, numbed now on the fence. He himself varied by all means, but as something, some rhythmic principle whose seat he rather thought was in the pit of his stomach. An almanac of his inconstancies was not unthinkable. But these women, positively it was scarcely an exaggeration to say that the four and twenty letters made no more and no more capricious variety of words in as many languages than they, their jigsaw souls, foisted on them that they might be damned, diversity of moods. Exaggeration or not, that was how it struck Belacqua, more forcibly now, as he adhered firmly to the fence and heard with great thankfulness the floes of shock crack in his heart-box, than perhaps ever before.

A quantity of phrases presented themselves to Zaborovna, who thus to her annoyance found herself faced with the alternative of saying nothing or preferring one.

'The garlic won't be worth eating' she said and at once repented her choice, as though she had had the least part in it, the pretty creature. So astute in some matters, so crass in others, so crass-astute in as many again, intruding like a flea her loose familiarities into the most retired places, how can she ever expect, as she does, to excel?

But now for it and like a lamb he followed her steps, up hill and down dale, to her lodging, where having arrived in the core of the darkest hour he at once devoured the garlic, tossed off the white rum, threw them thus mingled, after the manner of

Ninus the Assyrian, higgledy-piggledy on the stones, mentioned that he was bemired with sins, naked of good deeds and the meat of worms, and then to his astonishment was ravished, but ravished out of the horrid jaws agape for the lovefeast, the wrinkled gums and the Hutchinson fangs, which bit into nothing more fruity than what she afterwards described to a bosom pal as the dream of the shadow of the smoke of a rotten cigar, (1) just as the first sun opened a little eye in the heaven of blue Monday and gave light to a cock, ravished in the sense of reassumed, the first dose of resurgence having acted, into the lush plush of womby-tomby.

To proceed, after what seemed to Belacqua countless as it were eructations into the Bayswater of Elysium, brash after brash of atonement for the wet impudence of an earthly state – the idea being of course that his heart, not his soul but his heart, drained and dried in this racking guttatim, should qualify at last as a plenum of fire for bliss immovable – he appears to us again and more or less in the familiar attitude all set for his extraordinary affair with the spado in tail, if such a curious animal can be said to exist. Perched then on the lofty boundary of a simply enormous estate, guzzling a cheroot, the air filled with the camembert odours of goat, the stags belling fit to burst, tears for the betossed soul (his misnomer) flowing freely which was all to the good, he received such a stunning crack on his eminent coccyx, that little known funny bone of amativeness, that he all but swooned for joy. Never had he experienced such a tingling sensation, it was like having one's bottom skaterolled with knuckle-dusters.

1. The Voltigeur!

'Whoever you are' he cried, 'Jetzer or Juniperus —'

No answer.

'Firk away' he screamed, 'firk away, it is better than secret love.'

'Love' said a wearish voice behind him, 'turn round my young friend, face this way do, and tell me what you know of that disorder.'

Belacqua did as he was bid, because a little bird told him, do you see, that his hour had come and that it would be rather more graceful, not to say more sensible, to take it by the forelock, and looked down on a bald colossus, the Saint Paul's skull gathered into ropy dundraoghaires and a seamless belcher, dangling to and fro that help to holy living a Schenectady putter, clad in amaranth caoutchouc cap-à-pie, a cloak of gutta percha streaming back from the barrel of his bust, in his hand a gum tarboosh.

'I fear I caught you' said this strange figure 'with my last long putt. I got right under the beggar.'

'Then you have lost your ball' said Belacqua. 'What a shame!'

'I make my own' said the giant, 'I have some hundred thousand in a bag at home.'

'Where do you suppose' said Belacqua 'all this is leading to?'

'I am Lord Gall' said the colossus, 'if that means anything to you. Lord Gall of Wormwood. This is Wormwood. Possibility of issue is extinct.'

'Fecks' said Belacqua, 'never say die, the law won't.'

'The law is a ginnet' said Lord Gall. 'Did I ever tell you that one?'

'I may know it' said Belacqua, 'there aren't many I haven't forgotten at one time or another. But fire away.'

'It's a prime story' said Lord Gall, 'told me in a dream, or rather a vision. I'll communicate it as we go along.'

'Forgive me' said Belacqua, 'but go along whither?'

'By heaven' exclaimed Lord Gall, 'I have it all mapped out, believe me or believe me not. I don't know who you are, but that you will do me the hell of a lot of good I have little doubt. In fact I was thinking —'

Lord Gall blushed and could not go on. He tormented the tassel of his tarboosh. Belacqua urged him to conceal nothing.

'We are quite alone' he said 'except for a goat somewhere.'

'Well' said Lord Gall, 'I was thinking, if you did not mind, of addressing you in future as Adeodatus.'

He let fall the putter, settled the tarboosh firmly on his head, reached up with his arms and set Belacqua gently on the ground beside him.

'Take my hand' he said.

Timidly Belacqua made a little fist, placed in the monstrous bud, glowing with rings, of his patron, who suffered it to nestle there and even treated it to a long long fungoid squeeze that was most gratifying no doubt. Lord Gall stood, vibrating from head to foot, the cloak cracking like a banner, the sweat distilling through the caoutchouc in sudden stains, getting up steam in fact. Then abruptly he moved forward with a kind of religious excitement that jerked Belacqua clean off his feet.

'Steady' said Lord Gall.

Belacqua made a perfect landing and scuttled along in great style, a willing little pony.

'Now then' said Lord Gall. 'When our Lord —'

'Your putter sir' cried Belacqua, 'you have left it behind.'

'Pox on my putter' roared Lord Gall, vexed to the pluck, 'I have quiverfuls at home.'

Faster and faster they sped over the pasture, paved with edible mushrooms which Lord Gall scattered and spurned like a great elephant and big, Belacqua would have staked his reputation, with truffles. Yet he did not dare suggest that they should stop and fill their hankies.

'When our Lord' said Lord Gall, 'do you heed me?'

Belacqua felt that this was a piece of rhetoric. He was right.

'When our Lord' said Lord Gall for the third time 'stood in need of a mount and before the ass, to her undying credit, agreed unconditionally to carry him, he made overtures to the horse, who required notice of the question, and to the mule and ginnet, who bluntly refused.'

'The pigdogs!' cried Belacqua.

'Therefore' proceeded Lord Gall 'the Lord laid a curse on the mule and the ginnet, whose gist was that they should go no farther. With the twofold result that —'

'Primo' piped Belacqua.

'Primo: they have a glorious time. Secun —'

'In what sense' said Belacqua 'do they have a glorious time?'

As a train from a tunnel or a lady from a tank of warm water so now a wail, compound of impatience and rosy pudency, burst from the kidney-lipped maw of the raconteur.

'You hog's pudding' he cried, 'but inasmuch as they are not tenants in tail, what else?'

The oaths and groans of the unhappy man were happily to some extent drownded in a cyclone of wrath and disdain, something between the crowing of croop and a flushing-box doing its best, which at this juncture sprang up in his lights, bust all the bronchi, tattered the pleura, came thrashing and howling up his windpipe like an unclean spirit and left him quite breathless. But in his twenty-five stone of blubber, brawn, bone and bombast there was still ample motion to keep him going again his bellows should mend, which they very soon did he was thankful to say and did say.

'Secundo' said Mazeppa.

'Secundo' said Lord Gall, 'they can in no wise be translated into Gaelic.'

Belacqua applauded.

'Very nice' he said, 'witty but not vulgar, clean fun, a rare thing in this age. In a vision, did you say?'

Lord Gall, so used as to be impervious to blandishment, slackened speed and came gently to rest at the foot of a forest giant.

'My algum tree' he said. 'Highth – unknown; worth – not to be arrived at; girth – one half chain.'

'Under the bark?' said Belacqua.

'Under the bloody bark of course' said Lord Gall. 'Where did you think?'

Lord Gall, roused faintly, rub- rather than sud-orem being the ad quem, by such reiteration of 'oh please sir!' fatuity, flicked away the trusting hand of his tool as he might have a mosquito or the ash of a cigarette, sank his own thus freed into one of the many gnarls that adorned or marred the bole, one of those vulvate gnarls that Ruskin found more moving than even the noblest cisalpine medallions, pressed a button presumably for a deep slide-box, containing among an arsenal of strange objects that Belacqua could not for the moment identify a hogshead ale of hellebore, a double bass, a complete dry change and a full packet of photographs of Fräulein Dietrich, gushed forth with a piercing vagitus.

'My treasure' said Lord Gall simply, 'my own, my dear bowels.'

Lovingly he selected and secured a pair of brazen climbing-irons, slammed to the box by the superlative method of backing fiercely upon it with the bouncing bosses of the buckler of his bottom, remarking as he did do and without the least trace of affectation:

'That will be all for the present I rather fancy.'

'Certainly' said Belacqua. 'One thing at a time.'

But how he shuddered to think what that one thing might be!

'You talk wildly' said Lord Gall. 'Get you up on my neck.'

Before Belacqua had properly smoked this word of command and consequently long before the limbs of his body could begin to defer to it or otherwise, Lord Gall had ripped off his tarboosh (so designed that it could be telescoped like a crush hat and carried in the breast), flung himself down camel amuck, butted madly into the closed, nay folded, crutch of Adeodatus, pinned his ankles, swept him off the face of the earth in a nightmare pickaback and dashed up the tree.

Poor Belacqua, never longed his Mother so to see him first as now he, bursting with apprehension, for terra firma, some pleasant fence, the rhinal meditation, the private palpitation, the sense of sin and solid discomfort. Sedendo et quiescendo, yes, who said that? I came, I sat down, I went away, was that the ending end of all earthly sagacity, the cream, the quintessence and the upshot, or was it not? Little wealth, ill health and a life by stealth. But this, this rape, this contempt of his person, this violation of his postliminy, really it was not to be endured. In an unsubduable fit of pique he out with his razor and set to scalp Lord Gall, execrating him in the strongest terms the while.

'Drop that' said Lord Gall sharply, 'drop it this moment.'

Belacqua withheld his hand.

'Or I drop you' said Lord Gall, 'yes, like an oyster on the Aeschylus of Wormwood, pardon the reference.'

The top-gallant was lavishly appointed. Lord Gall discharged Belacqua into a cauldron of cushions, opened a bottle of Mumm, yes really opened a bottle of Mumm . . .

'To the hair on your chest' he said, 'forgive my brusqueness, my first name is Haemo don't you see, Haemo, so beastly plethoric, all this beef you see, these steaks and collops you may have noticed, my blasted blood boils and it's all up, I pledge you my word as apparently the last of the line I grovel before you, believe me or not sometimes I look on myself as utterly odious, I imprecate the hour I was got, with what gust I leave it to you to imagine, I —'

No doubt Lord Gall would have continued quite happily to patter up and down this crazy scantling of small chat far into the night were it not that a wind arose and shook the tree and rocked the crow's nest where they were and caused him thus to choke on a quick quinsy of alarm, greatly to the relief of Belacqua who began to feel as bruised in spirit as Richilda, relict of Albert, Duke of Ebersberg, in her happy little body, that is to say fatally. Lord Gall clung to the mast, Belacqua was tossed like a cork on his cushions, the furniture stampeded, a genuine Uccello flew out through the window. The wind dropped, the chamber quivered to rest and Belacqua, emboldened by

the spectacle of his oppressor spreadeagled like an O.H.M.S.
malefactor to the grating or triangles, said:

'State your business.'

Lord Gall came shamefacedly unstuck, sidled to an obviously secret drawer, mixed himself a stiff black velvet, knocked
it back, mixed himself another, flung it down, struck an attitude, quoted:

> 'The jealous swan against his death that singeth,
> And eke the owl that of death bode bringeth . . .',

mixed himself a third, tossed it off, lay down on his back on the
floor, drew up his knees and let them sag asunder in supreme
abandon, clasped his hands behind his head, coughed, spat,
missed, swore, apologised, belched, apologised, sneered and
stated his quandary in the following vigorous terms:

'You know who I am. I have and I hold in tail male special,
yes, tail male special, this Eden of Wormwood, one of the few
terrestrial Paradises outstanding in this country. While my
medical advisers assure me that I lack the power of procrea-
tion, my chaplains are good enough to condone this incapac-
ity as one that is natural, absolute, perpetual and antecedent.
My wife is a fruitful earth I have no doubt, albeit she harbours,
contracted in the alcove of the priapean Baron Extravas, protector under the instrument, reversioner of Wormwood and
fiend in human guise, the spirochaeta pallida.'

Lord Gall ceased, sat up, fumbled in his great patch fob,
drew out a mourning envelope containing ashes and dusted a
liberal sprinkling of these over his skull. Belacqua, crazed with
compassion, rolling about in a maffick of grief in his cauldron
or basket, felt it incumbent upon him to hazard a kind word:

'Disentail' he cried, 'bar it and hang the expense.'

Lord Gall cast up his arms, held them on high clenching and unclenching their hands, then set up, in deference no doubt to their aggrieved extensors, a fierce double-fisted attack on his breasts, knocked himself flat and said, or rather yelped:

'And kotow to the cad that peppered my love!'

He frothed at the blobbers.

'Adeodatus' he said, 'what is the sine qua non of every dirty deed of disentailment, answer me that.'

Belacqua was stumped.

'I give you up till ten' said Lord Gall, 'then I fire. One, two —'

Belacqua put on his considering cap.

'Four' said Lord Gall, 'five —'

'An official representation' said Belacqua 'of six or more villains.'

'Seven, eight' said Lord Gall, 'nine —'

'Or rather I should say' said Belacqua, 'the wink from the protector.'

'Very good' said Lord Doyle, 'and who is the protector here? Come now, answer up.'

'Baron Abore' said Belacqua, 'I think you said.'

'Wrong' said Lord Gall. 'Bend over.'

'Partepost' quavered Belacqua.

'Bend over' roared Lord Gall. 'Hold out your little bum here this instant.'

'Have pity' cried Belacqua, 'I have it.'

'You have not got it sir' thundered Lord Gall. 'You know you have not.'

'Extravas' said Belacqua. 'Keep your hair on.'

'Hair!' scoffed Lord Gall. 'Hair! Why my very dundraoghaires' passing his hands over his chaps and discovering their total impubescence 'are a concession to my station.' He put them back. 'For example, I have never known what it is to have hair on the head. All my life long, ever since I was – perish the day! – deprived of the breast, I have been as bald as a coot.'

Belacqua stood up in his basket.

'It is time I was getting on' he said.

Lord Gall took not the slightest notice, not the slightest.

'Very good' he said, 'Baron Extravas, that Frascatorian viper, do you imagine for one moment that he would agree to be barred in the eye or that I, Haemo Gall, backmarker in every form of athletic contest open to the peerage, would so far demean myself as to crawl to such an eversore? Pah!'

Belacqua hopped out of the basket or cauldron and squared up, dauntless little gamecock, to the aspermatic colossus, who upon the conclusion of his last outburst had sat up and wrapped his thighs about his face. That is my position, thought Belacqua, how dare he. Lord Gall peeped out.

'What is it now?' he said.

'Stand up' said Belacqua, 'be a little soldier, bite on the bullet.'

Lord Gall reeled to his feet and like a zebra began to act on the brainwave of more booze.

'Stop!' cried Belacqua. 'Don't be misled. Wine is a mocker.'

'Just one small tilly dawson' begged Lord Gall, 'and then I perish.'

'Why did the barmaid sham pain?' demanded Belacqua.

'Because the stout porter bit her' answered Lord Gall quite correctly.

'Very well' said Belacqua. 'You ask my advice. Here it is.'

'Make it short' said Lord Gall, 'facile, sweet and plain, I do beseech you.'

'As I see it' said Belacqua, 'the issue is perfectly distinct.'

'Extinct' said Lord Gall. 'However don't let me interrupt you.'

'One: no lives can be dropped. Two: you can't cut off the entail. Three: Wormwood reverts to the Baron.'

'Must you really go now?' said Lord Gall.

'Before I go —' said Belacqua.

'Excuse me' said Lord Gall, 'but have you made arrangements to be borne up on the way down?'

'Before I leave you' said Belacqua, 'there is just one word I should like to add. This yoke that is your portion, wear it lightly, do not let it wring your withers. Keep up your games, cultivate Wormwood in a good and husbandlike manner and according to local malfeasance, cherish Lady Gall, serve God, honour his assigns, early to bed, early to rise, fear no man, pray for the Baron, pray for me, good prayers and often for me if you would be so kind, keep up your pecker, stick to your games, transmit to posterity a name —'

'A name!' hooted Lord Gall. 'What name? Emptybreeks?'

So the battle raged, first one gaining the upper hand, then the other obtaining the advantage. Meantime the afternoon had not been idle, it had worn away, Belacqua thirsted for his quinquina. He had said that he would go and he was genuinely anxious to be gone, to fly away from Lord Gall, his tragic and oppressive presence. Unhappily the quomodo had yet to be contrived. He prayed for a Moby Dick of a miracle, but with so little conviction that he was not heard.

'Emptybreeks!' said Lord Gall. 'A name to conjure with.'

'Let us be serious' said Belacqua. 'We are getting what my dear tutor used to call no forrader.'

'Don't rip up old stories' said Lord Gall. 'Come to the point.'

'We all have our little afflictions' said Belacqua, 'they come to us all one and all sooner or later, if not to-day to-morrow or the day after, that is fatal. Yet I receive the impression that you put yourself forward as unique.'

'Come to the point' said Lord Gall.

'Look at me' said Belacqua. 'In virtue of the cruel rule that the image runs with the shadow, I am now precluded from looking into my eyes. I, Belacqua Shuah, Master of Arts, who spent my life between a bottle and a mirror, can no longer admire the front of my face. Yet I don't make a song about it. I put up with it. What can't —'

'Stop!' cried Lord Gall. 'Stop! Stop! Stop! Stop!'

'The old itch' said Belacqua 'to get in front of a mirror and then when there to wipe my face off it does more damage in five minutes than all the other pains and aches of the reversion in a week.'

'And yet you don't make a song about it' said Lord Gall.

'I do not' said Belacqua, 'I would scorn to.'

'The point' said Lord Gall, 'the point.'

'It is not enough to be continent —' said Belacqua.

'It most certainly is not' said Lord Gall. 'I believe you.'

'You must be sustenant also' said Belacqua, 'that is, titter affliction out of existence.'

'Christian' said Lord Gall with indescribable asperity 'bleeding science.'

'On the contrary' said Belacqua, 'these were the first self-supporting steps of thought in the west —'

'Saving a slight tendency to overwork the figure' said Lord Gall 'you phrase your ideas with distinction I should say.'

'My ideas!' exclaimed Belacqua. 'Really, my Lord, you forget that I am a postwar degenerate. We have our faults, but ideas is not one of them.'

'Well' said Lord Gall, 'yours or another's, proceed.'

'Men set them up —'

'What?' said Lord Gall. 'Set what up?'

'The steps of course' said Belacqua, 'set them up in every region of Magna Graecia, ascended to their apex of neutrality, found a comfortable position and drew them up —'

Lord Gall was really very dense. He could not follow the simplest discourse.

'What?' he said. 'Drew what up?'

'Why the steps to be sure' said Belacqua, 'drew them up after them.'

'Damn it all' said Lord Gall, 'they are sitting on them, how can they draw them up?'

'That is the point' said Belacqua. 'We have lost that faculty.'

'We certainly have' said Lord Gall, 'I believe you.'

'Yes' said Belacqua, 'ever since Socrates, the first great white-headed boy, with what delicious irony the whole world knows, turned up the tail of his abolla at the trees.'

Lord Gall pondered these strange things.

'Look at me' said Belacqua. 'Am I recalcitrant? Now I ask you.'

'In your own small way' said Lord Gall, 'I wouldn't put it past you.'

'Well well' said Belacqua, 'it's a strange world. And now I really must be off.'

Lord Gall stared out of the window.

'Off you hop' he said, 'don't wait for me.'

These cruel words left Belacqua no alternative but to dash himself heartily against the walls, happily padded, of the aerie. When thoroughly spent, but not a moment before, he said:

'Come come my lord, we are not children. Have the goodness to set me down. This is mere foolishness, my readers will be out of all patience.'

'Bide a wee' said Lord Gall.

'But I tell you I mot gon hoom' whined Belacqua, 'the sonne draweth weste.'

'Approach' said Lord Gall.

Belacqua, by now quite green, as green as Circe's honey, did not wait to be asked twice, and was rewarded for his alacrity by being caught up in the arms of his host or gaoler, who blew a box of asphodel off the window-sill and in its stead installed Belacqua. Poor Belacqua. Never did his mother . . . Lord Gall held him fast by the scruff of the pants.

'An ego jam sedeo?' said Belacqua. The rags of Latin flogged into us at school, in after life they stand to us well.

'Never mind about that now' said Lord Gall. 'What do you see?'

'A woolpack sky' said Belacqua, 'as beautiful as when I was a little boy.'

'What else?'

'Archipelagoes of pollards, spangled with glades.'

'Cut out the style' said Lord Gall. 'What else?'

'In the far distance a castle, and a young person, yes I venture to say a very charming young person, paddling in the moat.'

'Bully for you' said Lord Gall. 'My sweet column of quiet, partner of my porridge days, you ought to meet her.'

This possibility so entranced his lordship that for quite a time he could not go on with what he was saying. Belacqua was aware of the mouth opening and shutting behind (Lord Gall trying to go on and failing) and then, the angina of rapture dispersing, the pent up voice gushing into his ear-hole:

'Oughtn't you?'

'Cer'nly' said Belacqua, 'most happy to.'

'You know what I mean?' said Lord Gall.

'I think I can guess what you are driving at' said Belacqua.

'Good man' said Lord Gall, 'I bet you can. All this is vieux jeu. Now then, what else do you see?'

'Miles and miles of bright blue grass' said Belacqua.

'My champaign land' said Lord Gall blushingly, 'very prettily put.'

'Timberlike trees in great profusion' said Belacqua, 'brushwood in abundance and diadems of lakes.'

'Cut out the style' shouted Lord Gall, 'how often must I tell you?'

A crocodile, of men, and women, and children, passed slowly across a glade. Lord Gall obliged with a telescope, saying:

'Rose lens, my invention.'

Festooned with babies, the Smeraldina; a cynic in a spasm; a wedge of coisidte, fizzing through the future like a scoop through Stilton; a Nazi with his head in a clamp; a monster shaped like mankind exactly; Dáib and Seanacán, four legs in three tights and half a codpiece; a large Drumm pram, empty; the goat, confiding his chemical changes to Madam Frica, who derived such relish from the relation as was only superseded some days later, when she threw a party for a skunk; a tiny tot on her own. So they passed by and passed away . . .

'Well' said Lord Gall, when they had both quite done blowing their noses and wiping their eyes, or rather the other way about, 'what do you think of dear old Wormwood? Its animal life and vegetation? Does the little you have seen please you?'

'Immensely' said Belacqua, 'more than I can say. That pram I found most moving.'

'Excessively utile dulci' said Lord Gall, 'I vote for it every time. When the boy scouts get tired they lie down and wait for it to come up. You noticed its cutwater of course.'

Night fell like a lid.

'Most extraordinary thing!' exclaimed Belacqua.

Lord Gall lifted him off the sill, tossed him back into his cushions, closed the window, lit a candle, came over and sat down on the edge of the basket and began to speak with surprising sobriety.

'You have given me a great deal of trouble. Just consider: I take you off your fence, I tow you at high speed and no small pains across some of the finest country, I tell you one you didn't know, I let you have a peep at my treasure, I fly with you to my nest, I treat you to Mumm, I put up with your filthy bourgeois behaviour, I take you into my confidence, I endeavour to break down every barrier between us . . .'

Belacqua lighted a cigar at the candle but did not offer one to his benefactor.

'You have been most thoughtful and attentive' he said, 'I know. Don't you find the air up here rather close?'

'And that is all the thanks I get' said Lord Gall, 'a criticism of my own system of ventilation, my own patent, my very own. Oh Adeodatus!'

'I did not mean to be unkind' said Belacqua.

'Why do you suppose I have gone to all this trouble?' said Lord Gall. 'Can you think of no good reason?'

'I never care to look into motive' said Belacqua. 'It seems to be an impertinence. And that is a thing I have nearly done with.'

So the combat waxed and waned, each one giving to the other as good as he got. But is it not surely rather absurd that two reasonable men, on account of some purely capricious interdependence (as opposed to that relating the leprechaun, let us say, to the bleb, or Dáib to Seanacán), should insist on an act of contention that has, so to speak, consumed its bone, even as the fare that makes enemies of the best of friends never becomes a reality for the conductor? Still it may well be that we do them an injustice and that the bone is still there. Only time (if and when he eats it) can show.

'Now to move the limbs of the body' said Belacqua, 'now not; now to divide, multiply, contract, enlarge, order, disarrange, or in any other way image in the mind by thinking, now not – these are mysteries that I do not care to pry into. Neither Mary nor Martha can bubble me out of my deference, nor is it for me to say why Kant was not a cow. In fine, my Lord, I can do no more than thank you repeatedly, beseech you to put me back where you found me, or, if that is not convenient, at least on the right road, and ever remain your most humblecumdumble.'

Death does not seem to have improved Belacqua. Or are there perhaps signs of improvement? Yes and no.

'It is not a question' said Lord Gall 'of what you can or of what you can not do. That point is one that will doubtless arise later. For the moment it will be quite enough for you to do as you are told. Prepare therefore to receive your instructions.'

Belacqua lay aside the cigar and smartened himself up in the cauldron.

'I may mention' said Lord Gall 'that it was in my contemplation, until your latest flux of bilge abolished it, to make you a more than liberal offer on account of your services.'

'I am no longer for sale' said Belacqua, 'being now incorruptible, not to mention uninjurable, while my margin of changeability is of the narrowest.'

'That is perfect' said Lord Gall, 'because this night, after the manner of all the earth, in you go unto my lady, who shall toe the scratch I don't doubt for a moment and call his name Haemo.'

'Oh' said Belacqua, 'you puddle of iniquity! Would you have me made a father? Shameful spewing on your glory!'

Lord Gall, whose movements could not be forecast from one moment to another, now began to stab back and forth with his clubbed index, speaking almost pidgin:

'You' (stab) 'makee me' (stab) 'father.'

'And Lady Gall?' said Belacqua, who was a modest fellow and thought that every lady was entitled to select her own vestryman.

'Leave Moll to me' said Lord Gall, 'leave the whole timetable to me.'

'And if I decline' said Belacqua, 'which you are bound to admit would be only human flesh and blood, after the details you have given me?'

'Then' said Lord Gall, very Olympian (or perhaps better Olympic) all of a sudden, 'then I shall never speak to you again, but rather drop all my games, take to the bottle and die in the rats intestate.'

'Picking at the bed-clothes' said Belacqua, 'what?'

Lord Gall sulked.

'Bless you' said Belacqua, 'don't despair. Hungry dogs eat dirty puddings.'

Lord Gall brightened up considerably.

'My experience too' he said. 'Very prettily put I should think.'

'Shall we chafe' inquired Belacqua 'that our age is that of a fly? Or a cock? Is there more God in an elephant than in an oyster?'

'Exactly the same amount' said Lord Gall, 'I should have thought.'

'The same quota exactly' said Belacqua. 'Then why worry?'

At this point they joined in singing Oh les femmes et les framboises, they felt they simply had to, to the glory of the non-spatial divinity.

'You sing beautifully' panted Belacqua. 'I declare to God you centre your notes like a lepidopterist.'

'Say rather an invisible seamstress' said Lord Gall. (A very poor effort by the way.) 'What will you take?'

'Pernod' said Belacqua, 'now that we're in Paris, Père, Fils and Saint Esprit.'

'I'm out of Pernod' said Lord Gall, 'but the Fernet Branca is in nice order.'

'I'll try half a pint' said Belacqua. 'Pour it high.'

When they had quite drunk to the perdition of Extravas (Belacqua: 'Why has the Lord not put it across him?' Lord Gall: 'Ask me an easier one.') and to a happy issue (Both: 'Ach Kinder!') out of their manifold afflictions (Lord Gall: 'You are sure that this will not prove too much for you? You are sure you would not care for a few oysters?' Belacqua: 'No, thank you. I find them rather, indeed altogether, too succulent.'), and almost before the liquor had had time to decide in which direction, up or down, it was going, Lord Gall burst his banks as follows:

'But by God I am sick and tired of this endless conversation,' set to and swept and garnished the aerie, seized Belacqua in his arms, opened a trap-door in the flooring, went through it, prehended the bole beneath with magnificent thighs, let his trunk fall back parallel to what Belacqua could only think of as the celestial horizon, whistled and sped earthwards, in a cataclasm of boughs and a moonlit pandemonium of autumn tints. When he got there he opened his cupboard and took out a tin.

'Vaseline' he said, 'omnia vincit.'

He lashed it on in great style.

'Inunction' he said 'for my exanthem, and – handy-dandy! – I feel as fit as a flea.'

Belacqua recovered consciousness.

'Windfalls of sound timber' he heard Lord Gall, in apostrophe of the gross waste he had committed, cry from afar off, 'I weep to see, and so will the reversioner in all likelihood.'

Lord Gall had the reversioner on the brain.

Belacqua spewed. Dimly he seemed to discern the tree trunk yawn and disclose an extensive mew, from the depths of which, where it had been lurking, a rogue ostrich, of all unexpected objects, came forward at the bidding of Lord Gall.

'Meet Strauss' said Lord Gall. 'He simply waltzes along, never hesitates. Oopsadaisy.'

If this injunction applied to Strauss, who had begun to bury his head in the ground, it applied doubly to Belacqua, for he lay there as one dead. Complying in any case promptly

together they came into contact, the crutch and thighs of the
man, or rather ghost, with the priceless boa of the bird, upon
whose scarcely less valuable rump Lord Gall distributed himself, in the happy position of being able to brake with his feet
on the ground their flight should it wax too headlong. Strauss
sagged and murmured something that sounded remarkably
like 'Struth!'

'Silence!' cried Lord Gall. 'Silence at once! Forward.'

'Before we start' said Belacqua, 'there is just one thing.'

Lord G. pawed the ground.

'For one who does not care to pry into mysteries' he said,
'you show great enterprise I must say.'

Such a speech! Really Lord Gall . . . !

'Lady Gall' began Belacqua.

'Call her Moll' said Lord Gall.

'Is she —' stammered Belacqua, 'would she —'

'Damme she DOES' roared Lord G. 'The whole success of
our enterprise turns about her doing so.'

'You take me up too fast' said Belacqua, 'wait for the
question.'

Lord G. leaned forward and mollified his mount.

'Strauss' he said, 'I must beg of you to wait. Something is
galling the weight on your neck.'

'Would she sink or swim in Diana's well?' said Belacqua. 'Yes
or no?'

'Sink' said Lord Gall.

'Oh' said Belacqua, 'I can't tell you how glad I am to hear that.'

'I think' said Lord Gall, 'sink I think. Wait for the answer.
Forward.'

In less time than it takes to decide how this tedious episode

may best be liquified they reached the castle, poor Strauss
very bedraggled and inclined to mope. Lord Gall took charge
of everything, Belacqua had merely to go in unto. Moll turned
out to be the most filthy little bromide of a half-baked puella
that you could possibly imagine, face like a section of spanked
bottom, simple duple specks, giggle, clitoridian croon, warts
and a cacoethes of hoisting all propositions addressed to her,
or such passages from them as she did not find obscure, and a
large number of those that were not, a couple of pegs with great
enthusiasm and conviction. (1) Anyhow in he went, executed
himself with a kind of wild civility and then, before she had
nearly exhausted her Leaving Certificate ta-ta! for his super,
simply ripping, perfectly topping attentions, was lapped in the
Lethe of another truce, restored in a twinkling to the fence of
integrity and thence without pause to his base, the uterotaph.

That seems to be about the end of the adventure of the
impotent tenant in tail male special, unless it might tickle
the reader, as it did the Baron greatly, to learn that Moll Gall
turned up trumps and was brought to bed amidst scenes of
the wildest enthusiasm, and that on the tick of the fulness of
time a life was dropped. Lord Gall was downstairs at the time,
counting his golfballs. His medical advisers filed in. It was a
dramatic moment.

'May it please your lordship' said the foreman, 'it is essentially a girl.'

So it goes in the world.

1. E.g.: lady gall: Diddleumdumdum diddlediddleumdum diddle-
diddle —
belacqua: It is now three o'clock in the morning.
lady gall: (vehemently) Rather! Absolutely! Jolly good! Diddlediddleum
dumdiddleum etc.

To proceed then again more or less as see above, page 7,
paragraph 2, Belacqua, at last on the threshold of total extinction as a free corpse, sat on his own headstone, drumming his
heels irritably against the R.I.P. What with the moon shining,
the sea tossing in her sleep and sighing, and the mountains
observing their Attic vigil in the background, he found it difficult to decide offhand whether the scene was of the kind that
is called romantic or whether it should not with more justice
be termed classical. Both elements were present, of that there
could be no question. Perhaps classico-romantic would be the
fairest diagnosis. A classico-romantic scene.

Personally, he felt calm and wistful. A classico-romantic
corpse.

He brought up duly the words of the rose to the rose: 'No
gardener has died, within rosaceous memory.'

He sang a little song, he could not help and that was all
about it, nor can we refrain from setting it down, however ill it
suit with this deep witty story.

> *Ich liebe Dich, Titine,*
> *Ich muss Dich ewig lieben,*
> *Denn Du bist die Rosine*
> *In meines Lebens Kuchen.*

He sighted a submarine of souls on the sea, hove to, casting
– no, drawing up a net. He counted the fish as the Alba, coiled
up on the conning tower, sporting the old flamingo, gaffed
them and brought them on board, one by one. One hundred
and fiftythree iridiscent fish, the sum of the squares of Apostles and Trinity, thrashing and foaming on the gaff. He closed
his eyes, intending to have a vision, but felt so marooned when

he did so that he opened them again quick. The boat was gone.

The significance of this apparition was what he could not fathom. No, nor anyone else either.

Cats came and sat down. In their faces, wreathed in tolerance, he blew the smoke of his last cigar, hoping thus to shift them. But they continued to come and sit down and surrounded him on all sides finally. He supposed he was all right so long as he stayed where he was. But woe betide him presumably if he tried to sneak away.

The next item on the programme turned out to be our old friend the groundsman, whom we did not bother to name in Draff, but now must: Doyle was his name.

Belacqua was glad to see him.

'My old friend Mick' he said.

This man Doyle was naked save for his truss and a pair of boots which sparkled and crackled in the moonlight. He wore tatooed in block capitals of fire, a flaming zoster across his tumtum, the words: Stultum Propter Christum. He carried a clothes-basket, a dark lantern, a mattock, an axe, a shovel, a spade and a hamper. With a shoulder-elbow-palm-and-eyebrow ikey most pleasing to see he washed as it were his hands of all this baggage which consequently clattered to the ground, floundered around in a wild romp or perhaps better flurry and lay still. The cats faded away.

'Mick doesn't know Bel' said Belacqua, 'what a shame.'

Doyle went away and came back, sorted his tools, raised the mattock on high and observed merely, in a Dublin accent of great sweetness:

'Don't you imagine that you, who are a patent figment, can put the wind up me, who am fortified with alcohol.'

Down came the mattock on the hallowed mould like the pile-driver in the story, such a blow can seldom have been delivered, the headstone rocked, Belacqua's last resting-place spouted up into his eye.

'Easy on there' said Belacqua, 'what's the big idea?'

'The idea' said Doyle, developing his vile work with the energy, skill and despatch of a model machine-moujik, '– is – in a word – to snatch.'

'Fool' said Belacqua.

'And grab' said Doyle.

'Fool' said Belacqua, 'I am the body.'

Doyle threw down the mattock and took up the spade.

'There is a natural body' he said 'and there is a spiritual body.'

He laid down the spade, went away and came back, he took up the shovel.

'Reach hither with your shovel' said Belacqua.

But Doyle apparently had no interest in being convinced, for he went on with his work in a dogged and a sullen manner. He was a good worker, already he had quite a little cavity to his credit. He laid down the shovel and resumed the mattock. Belacqua spat in his eye, saying:

'Is that also a figment?'

This was indeed an impardonable piece of interference and yet Doyle took it as the vagabond in Walking Out the blue bitch's affront, that is without visible rancour, plying his tool, a dunderhead, a sweet dolt on some Christ's account.

'I'll lay you six to four' said Belacqua 'that you find nothing.'

Doyle laid down the mattock, he went away and came back, he stood irresolute in the midst of clothes-basket, shovel, spade and hamper, mass of inertia in pentacle of delirium.

'Two to one' said Belacqua, 'five to two, I lay five to two.'

Doyle plumped for the spade, discovered his mistake, sought to retrieve it with the shovel, in vain, with the clothes-basket, too late the damage was done, stood helpless and disarmed, on the verge of a breakdown.

'Hear me' implored Belacqua.

Doyle's wild eye saw the hamper, he fell upon it, devoured the wing of a chicken, opened a bottle not of stout but of schnapps.

'Oh Mick hear me!'

Doyle, utterly dispirited by the hitch in his work, regretting the wing of the chicken already, acutely conscious that the schnapps was not going to the right place, the slow climb of flat themes like a bougie in his brain (some were of the opinion that Doyle was mad), realised that there was nothing further to be gained from withholding his attention. So he just said agreeably:

'These amethyst bottles are a great mistake. They don't give the drink a fair chance to my mind.'

'In this world' said Belacqua, 'which, as you know, is all temptation and commercial travelling, I contrived, notwithstanding my numerous wives and admirers, to pass the greater share of my time in the privy, papered in ultraviolet anguish, of my psyche, projecting diggings so deep that their intrigues should never be discovered until a grandson's natural monster had forgotten me, my peccadilloes of omission.'

Doyle knew the class of thing exactly, the sense of inertness in leash, pent up sluggishness. It seemed to thrive, more was the pity, on his line of business.

'Don't I know' he said. 'You may pass on to the next section.'

An icy wind, harbinger of the dawn, began to blow. Belacqua, observing how little by little Doyle was turning blue, resolved piously to be as brief as possible.

'As amber attracts chaff' he said, 'so my psyche —'

'If you would be so kind' said Doyle 'as to make use of the word mind, because the word psyche reminds me in the first place of the Irish Statesman and in the second place of a girl who used to know me.' His voice came to pieces. 'Long ago' he sobbed.

'Gladly' said Belacqua. '. . . attracts chaff, so my mind all the stupefying dilemmas. Until, my anaesthesia becoming general, I was called home, to adopt the happy expression of Mr Quin whom you may have met, at last. To my last long home at long last. Since when the sty, saving your presence, which I in my childish way supposed would see me no more, has claimed so much of my time that I sometimes wonder whether death is not the greatest swindle of modern times.'

Without the slightest hesitation Doyle made a mot of some note.

'For the purposes of stinging' he said 'Death is no better equipped than a wasp.'

Belacqua thought it very good but did not say so. He made a mental note of it however. He knew exactly on whom he could place it with most success. He went on with his own stuff.

'Now is not the whole thing rather peculiar? I who was always as quiet as a mouse, doing nothing, saying nothing, my mind a Limbo of the most musical processes, to be treated now as though I had been on the committee.'

Doyle went away. Belacqua, the phrases to come next piping hot in his mind, counted the moments until he should return. The submarine kept bobbing up and down, nearer to the shore at each emergence. To little Alba, waving from the conning tower and beckoning in a most unladylike manner, Belacqua vouchsafed no sign. Yet he bore the whole manoeuvre in mind, resolved to exploit it should occasion arise. After what seemed a lifetime Doyle came back, greatly eased to judge by his tranquil expression.

'Is it not rather peculiar?' said Belacqua.

'Scarcely just' said Doyle 'let alone equitable.'

'I find it difficult to imagine' said Belacqua 'any rightminded person failing to be shocked at such disparity between merit and requital.'

His imagination is certainly not what it was.

'How do you figure it out?' said Doyle.

'I dassay my life was a derogation and an impùdence' said Belacqua 'which it was my duty, nay should have been my pleasure, to nip in the wombbud. But —'

'Half a mo' said Doyle. 'You say derogation. From what?'

'Really' said Belacqua, 'consideration for your cyanosis forbids me to go into that. Also I have the feeling that time is short, a kind of aura if I may say so.'

Doyle sighed.

'I do think you might tell me' he said.

'Aren't you a perfect little pest' cried Belacqua, 'wanting to know everything. Who but an imbecile can care from what? Isn't derogation in the dear old abstract good enough?'

Doyle, silent and inclined to brood, gave the false impression that he did not think so, that he had the very lowest opinion of the abstract, false because his mind was dwelling on something quite different. He was thinking that perhaps it might be wise to run back for his trowel.

'If it's good enough for me' shouted Belacqua 'isn't it too good for you? There you glump like a fluke in a tup and want to know from what. Can you think of any thing existing, God or Gonococcus, lower than the creature, his three score years and ten of hot cockles?'

Doyle, deep down in his heart, felt this to be an overstatement. But he knew that it would never do to say that. Doyle was a natural man of the world.

'Réchauffé cockles' he said.

This little effort, worthy of the Communist painter and decorator in his palmiest days, transported Belacqua and caused him to ejaculate:

'Hah! There she spouts, the Mick I know, the great greedy wild free human heart I know!'

'"But"' said Doyle, 'you were saying "but —"'

'My memory has gone to hell altogether' said Belacqua. 'If you can't give me a better cue than that I'll have to be like the embarrassed caterpillar and go back to my origins.'

Doyle did not smoke the reference.

'He was working away at his hammock' said Belacqua, 'and not doing a damn bit of harm to man or beast, when up comes old Monkeybrand bursting with labour-saving devices. The caterpillar was far from feeling any benefit.'

Bear in mind that all this time Doyle had been going away and coming back, ostentatiously eased, as regular as clockwork.

'What ails you Mick?' said Belacqua not unkindly.

Doyle however would not brook even the most courteous attention to be drawn to his weakness and so he just blushed through the blue and rapped out the following reminder, yes really rapped it out:

'You were mentioning how that though' – surely a rather unusual construction? – 'as a foetus you erred, yet —'

'Ah yes to be sure' said Belacqua, 'thank you Mick', and fell into rêverie as though time were of no consequence.

After a long silence, suffered by Doyle as scarcely less than a tribute to his high-class folly, something inside Belacqua said for him:

'Sometimes he feels as though this old wound of his life had no intention of healing.'

'That sounds bad' said Doyle, 'I grant you. Has he tried saline?'

'He has tried everything' said the voice 'from fresh air and early hours to irony and great art.'

'And obtained no relief?'

The thought of not being able to obtain relief sent Doyle flying. When he came back the voice admitted that great art had proved a great boon while it lasted.

'But he couldn't stand the pace' it sighed, 'the counter irritation was something terrific.'

Belacqua passed his hand over his face.

'How do I look?' he said.

'Your eyes are full of tears' said Doyle, 'positively flooded my poor friend.'

'I didn't mention' said Belacqua, 'or did I, that all reflectors of what kind soever have cast me off. Yes. They cut me now. I don't exist for them. I remember the first time —'

'If you will mewl without ceasing' said Doyle, 'what else can you expect?'

'Twas on an Ash Wed-nes-day —'

'I declare to me God' said Doyle, 'you wear me to the pith with your —'

'With my what?' said Belacqua. 'What does poor Bel wear Mick to the pith with?'

'How shall I say?' said Doyle. 'Shall I say with the eccentricities of your conversation, your buckled discourse? You must be rotten through and through to fly out of your own system the way you do. Stick to the point, honour your father, your mother and Göthe. Do I make myself at all clear?'

'Bright as light and clear as wind' said Belacqua.

'Good' said Doyle. 'Now are you right now, are you all set to take over?'

'Keyed up' said Belacqua. 'I'll snap in a second.'

'That first, fatal, foetal' said Doyle, sitting down inexorably on all the commas, 'error, or, better, blunder, notwithstanding —'

Dead silence.

'Go ON' shrieked Doyle, 'don't pick, play a card curse you!'

'Comma' said Belacqua, 'notwithstanding, comma, yes, blunder, better still, comma, notwithstanding, two dots, yes, ha —'

Inhuman cry.

'What was that?' cried Belacqua.

Another and another. Doyle, Doyle, his head flung back, his throat olive convulsed, was making them. Up they came, bubbling from his belly, with whose awful heaving the scarlet slogan was in entire sympathy. He could not go on making them and live, Belacqua did not need to have been bumped off by a Fellow of some Royal College of Surgeons to see that. He made seven in all and then he stopped. Another three would have counted him out.

'What you need' said Belacqua 'is perfect quiet and darkness.'

Horror! It was dawning.

'For one gentleman' said Belacqua 'with a fusilade of amplified death-rattles to intrude upon another in the very ecstasy of his peroration seems to be the act of a cad and a curdog. I stand open to correction.'

'The two dots' panted Doyle, 'they seemed to scorch me like hell-fire.'

Dawn, aborting all over the layette of night. Pfui!

'When you are quite ready' said Belacqua, 'recovered, almost your old self again, then I have hopes of proceeding, under one, two and three, to bury this demented conversation. But not until you are quite ready, not a moment before.'

'One, two, three' groaned Doyle. 'God forgive you.'

'One' said Belacqua: 'I shall make a statement; two, I shall make a suggestion; three, I shall aid you to act upon it, with or without modifications, or, bist Du nicht willig, bid thee farewell.'

'Bating Chinese corkscrews in my skull' said Doyle, 'I feel A.I.'

Belacqua settled himself more comfortably, i.e. more thighs and less rump, on the headstone, and began:

'One: scarcely —'

'Bear with me' murmured Doyle.

'What do you say?' said Belacqua. 'Don't be so beastly inaudible.'

'Is it de rigueur' said Doyle, 'the crazy old chronology? One, two, three. Why people have not got the gumption to begin with the Dove and end up with the Son passes my persimmon.'

'I dare not' said Belacqua, 'much as I should like to, put the cart before the horse in this particular case.'

'Well if you can't' said Doyle, going away and coming back, 'you can't. The horse, the cart, and then – ?'

'Then haply the deluge' said Belacqua. 'And keep your bake shut now or I'll fly away with you.'

'Game ball' said Doyle.

The vagabond again! Dear oh dear oh dear! The good old pastoral days, prior to Thanatos.

'One' said Belacqua, 'scarcely had my cord been clumsily severed than I struggled to reintegrate the matrix, nor did I relax those newborn efforts until death came and undid me.'

'But did it?' said Doyle.

'It is doing so' said Belacqua, 'it cannot go any faster.'

'And it is on that basis' said Doyle, 'in consideration of a life-time of gaudy prenatal velleities, that you deem that death has done the dirty on you?'

'I did feel' said Belacqua, 'I must admit I did feel that I was being hardly used. But that impression, I am happy to say, has since been corrected.'

'Why then – ?' said Doyle.

'I should really greatly prefer not to go into that question' said Belacqua. 'Economy is the great thing now, from now on till the end.'

'Then let us have the cart' said Doyle. 'The old stars are like stains of dew.'

'Two' said Belacqua, 'I lay you the most fabulous odds that nothing of me subsists in this grave. Not a ring, not a hair, not the crown of a tooth, not a nail, not a bone. Is that a bet or do we part?'

'Make it three to one' whined Doyle, 'cantcher? A half-dozen of stout to a nice pint.'

'Done' said Belacqua. 'Better a gull than a Protestant Gael.'

'In the event of dispute' said Doyle, 'it might be a wise thing to appoint an arbitrator. My terrace teems with archaeologists, any one of whom I happen to know would be more than happy to act.'

More than happy! What an expression for a man in Doyle's position.

'What dispute can conceivably arise between gentlemen?' said Belacqua. 'Have a little sense Doyle.'

Doyle ate dirt.

'Thank you Doyle' said Belacqua.

'Shall I grovel now' said Doyle, 'or are you appeased.'

'That will do nicely' said Belacqua. 'I am not a jealous person.'

'Then three' said Doyle.

'To work' cried Belacqua, 'and may the better man win!'

'My hand on that' exclaimed Doyle with much heartiness.

Thus it was that Doyle, slush though he was of incuriosity, did after all reach forth. Sooner or later, willing or unwillingly, they all do. There are no exceptions to this rule, take it or leave it.

Consequently in the dawn dust of a dove's heart descending after her pains to arrive they fell to and that with such a will, Doyle revelling in the glow of exertion, Belacqua in a fever of curiosity naturally, that the long lid of Nichol's box, its handsome finish rather thrown away in the mire and gloom of the pit, in next to no time amply repaid them. But behind their backs the sea had developed the stippled contexture of hammered lead, very saturnine, and the submarine, plunging up and down madly in the shallows, an agitato that entered the corner of Belacqua's eye as an admonition not to dally.

'Many hands make light work' said Doyle complacently, kneeling on the box, wiping the last clots of muck from the lid with a damp clout, wondering what on earth had possessed him to tackle such a job alone, at his time of life, with his increasing physical disabilities. Then unexpectedly he clapped his hand to where he felt his heart beating, not far from the armpit. Was he going to have a seizure, that was the interesting question.

'Misery!' he cried. 'I forgot the turnascrew.'

But Belacqua, persuaded that there was not a moment to lose, cried out a curse on all turnascrews, snatched up the axe and dealt the coffin such a welt as laid it open from stem to stern, shivering all its brass bands and catapulting Doyle into the adjoining plot sacred to the memory of one Gottlob. Doyle, on whom the long night of knock-about was beginning to tell and small wonder, rose to his feet very groggy, all the wind taken out of him, and went away needless to say. Belacqua parted the frilled cerements and peeped inside to see what he could see. But what with the dark and the dank vapours blurring his glasses he could see nothing and he felt the same reluctance to thrust in his hand and grope as all hypersensitive people do at the thought of retrieving some precious object, a locket or a coin, from say an earth-closet. So he just sat tight until Doyle came back and then called out to him to pass down his lantern.

'Certainly' said Doyle, 'of course.'

'Yes' said Belacqua, 'show a glim, there's a dear fellow, I'm blinded.'

Doyle kneeled on the lip of the excavation and lowered the lantern. Suddenly he was Adam that good old man, trembling with loyalty and constant service, though no sympathetic metamorphosis we regret to say was evinced by Belacqua, who sniffed and said:

'Do you smell the tubers?'

Doyle could not honestly say that he did.

'Light and sweetness' said Belacqua, 'Sweetness and Light, Obliterate dole, And engender delight.'

'Bravo' said Doyle.

'And whoso lacks these shall consume like a spider away.'

Belacqua threw open the shutter of the lantern and the light streamed over his face.

'Fortunate candle!' he cried, 'you might be greasing the palm of some saint this minute.'

He cocked up the yellow beam at Doyle.

'You don't look well at all Doyle' he said, 'with your scalped belly.'

As he turned and stooped to investigate his remains (if any) it occurred to him that he was at the mercy of this strange sexton or groundsman or whatever you like to call him, so advantageously placed above and behind him, all manner of lethal implements to his hand, and rage in his heart as likely as not. Consequently it was in a state of some trepidation that he extirpated the rank shroud, coaxed the lantern into the coffin and played its yellow eye in all directions. As for the unhappy Doyle, all that he could see was the peering bulk of the inquirer and an inconsiderable section of the coffin's interior, where the alternation of dim flashes with periods of total obscuration entered his consciousness, for he was rather too ecstatically disposed at this crisis to associate his impressions in a reasonable way, like the frolics of a toy moon in a toy storm. Then abruptly the ubiquitous flickering resolved itself into a steady tremolo of light over a small area, narrowing and brightening, the area not the tremolo, as Belacqua poked forward the lantern at his find.

'Give it a name' said Doyle in a voice that he had some difficulty in recognising.

What a scene when you come to think of it! Belacqua petrified link-boy, the scattered guts of ground, the ponderous anxiomaniac on the brink in the nude like a fly on the edge of a sore, (1) in the grey flaws of tramontane the hundreds of headstones sighing and gleaming like bones, the hamper, mattock, shovel, spade and axe cabal of vipers, most malignant, the clothes-basket a coffin in its own way, and of course the prescribed hush of great solemnity broken only by the sea convulsed in one of those dreams, ah one of those dreams, the submarine wallowing and hooting on the beach like an absolute fool, and dawn toddling down the mountains. What a scene! Worthy of Mark Disney.

Belacqua's immobility began to prey on Doyle, who craned down, collapsed gargoyle, into the void.

'A little Goldwasser' he urged, 'direct from Danzig.'

Poor Belacqua, the best he could do by way of response to this kind offer was a lightning shudder, like a zip fastener it rattled down the slats of his spine. He was properly buttoned up this time. And poor Doyle too, we don't forget him, all poor people we don't forget them, in a chaos of spirit he fell tooth

1. Indeed there was more than a little of the gardener in Draff about Doyle.

and nail on the hamper, tore forth the jar, fairy jar, sausage balloon, bit off its fragile neck, yes really seemed to bite it off, drained in a frenzy its cordial contents, essence of flecked pupil of women adored in secret, and went away.

The Alba said in a general way:

'Shall we tarry here until perdition catch us?'

The passengers agreed that that would be a mistake.

'Have we not gone out of our way' she said 'to do the right thing, the kind thing?'

'Miles out of our course' said the passengers.

'What thanks do we get?' said the Alba.

The passengers were beginning to cotton on.

'Small thanks' they cried.

'To hell with him so' said the Alba.

So the submarine departed, very cross indeed.

In the coffin the handful of stones that Belacqua had found, the lantern lying on its side, the sweet smell of tubers killed in the snuff of candle.

The cemetery a cockpit of comic panic, Doyle stalking and rushing the tombstones, squatting behind them in ambush, behaving in a way quite foreign to his nature.

So it goes in the world.

ANNOTATIONS

The following abbreviations have been used for frequently cited texts; full details of editions used are found in the bibliography.

Augustine   St Augustine: *Confessions*

Burton   Robert Burton: *The Anatomy of Melancholy*

Cooper   William M. Cooper: *Flagellation and the Flagellants*

CP   Samuel Beckett: *Collected Poems*

Dis   Samuel Beckett: *Disjecta*

DN   Beckett's *Dream* Notebook, with entry number

Dream   Samuel Beckett: *Dream of Fair to Middling Women*

Garnier   Pierre Garnier: *Onanisme seul et à deux sous toutes ses formes et leurs consequences*

Giles   H. A. Giles: *The Civilisation of China*

Lockhart   J. G. Lockhart: *The History of Napoleon Bonaparte*

LSB I   Samuel Beckett: *The Letters of Samuel Beckett, vol. 1: 1929–1940*

LSB II   Samuel Beckett: *The Letters of Samuel Beckett, vol. 2: 1941–1956*

MPTK   Samuel Beckett: *More Pricks Than Kicks*

OED   *The Oxford English Dictionary*

Renard   Jules Renard: *Le Journal de Jules Renard 1887–1910*

Taylor   Jeremy Taylor: *The Rule and Exercises of Holy Living and Holy Dying*

TCD   Trinity College Dublin

UoR   University of Reading

Roman numerals relate to book and chapter, or act and scene of the cited work. No specific page number is given for books that are available in multiple editions. All citations from the Bible are from the Authorised King James Version.

Title: taken from Ovid's *Metamorphoses* (III, l. 399), as noted in
   DN: 'Echo's bones were turned to stone' (1101). Her love for
   Narcissus unrequited, Echo pines away until only her voice
   and her bones remain.
'shafts': cf. 'shafts of emergal' in *Dream* (16).
'back into the muck': a commonplace and persuasive description
   of the world in the Beckett canon. He was fond of the line 'the
   world is dung' ('e fango e il mondo') in Giacomo Leopardi's
   'To Himself' ('A se stesso'), a poem Beckett typed out in the
   1930s (TCD MS10971/9).
'lord of the manor': together with 'trespass', 'acquiescence' and 'duty
   of care', forms the legal terminology of this first sentence, and
   anticipates the legal issue of Lord Gall's estate later in the text.
'free among the dead': based on St Augustine's *Confessions* (IX,
   xiii); as noted in *DN*, Christ was '"free among the dead" – He was
   the only Dead free from the debt of Death' (180; cf. also *Dream*
   86). As Augustine goes on to say, having laid down his life, Christ
   is able to take it up again, reflecting Belacqua's return from the
   dead. The phrase 'free among the dead' also occurs in Psalm 88.
'debt of nature': death, although in Christian terms this is usually
   seen as the result of sin, and thus not strictly a 'debt of nature'.
'post-obit': Latin 'after death'. Usually used as a legal term to
   designate an outstanding issue (often a debt) that takes effect
   after death.
'estate': anticipates the issue of Lord Gall's estate in the second
   part of the story.
'same stream twice': Heraclitus on the unchanging thrust of
   time; Beckett read texts by and about Heraclitus in the early

1930s. Cf. Beckett's 'Philosophy' Notebook: 'For him it is
not possible to step down twice into the same stream'
(TCD MS10967, 24r). The idea reappears for example in
the poem 'For Future Reference' (*CP* 28), the essay
'Le Monde et le Pantalon' (*Dis* 118) and the postwar story 'The
Expelled' (9).

'a true saying': found in *Dream* (40), twice in 'Dante and Lobster'
and in 'Yellow' (*MPTK* 8, 17, 163).

'Belacqua': Beckett's earliest protagonist, the 'hero' of *Dream*
and *MPTK*, based on the Florentine lute-maker of the same
name in Dante's *Divine Comedy*. Confined in purgatory for
indolence, Dante encounters him crouching in the shade of
a great rock (*Purgatorio* IV, 127). Asked by Dante why he is
sitting rather than ascending the Mount of Purgatory, Belacqua states, 'Brother what avails it to ascend?', believing that
he would surely not be allowed to enter Paradise. Notes on
Dante's Belacqua can be found in *DN* (305, 311, 313, 314, 315). Cf.
also the boy in the poem 'Enueg I', who refrains from trying to
watch the hurling game.

'dust of the world': as in the Book of Job, 'will thou bring me into
dust again' (10:9), or a line from Proverbs (8:26) noted in *DN*:
'the highest part of the dust of the world' (553). Cf. *Dream* (31,
78) and 'What a Misfortune' (*MPTK* 115).

'dim spot' – i.e. 'Earth', as defined by the attendant Spirit in Milton's *Comus* (ll. 6–7).

'not all a dream': one of several allusions to the 'source' text
which underlies 'Echo's Bones', the (then) unpublished *Dream
of Fair to Middling Women*.

'quick': cf. 'the quick and the dead' (I Peter 4:5).

'definite individual existence . . . order of time': Beckett is here
liberally quoting Anaximander from Friedrich Ueberweg's *History of Philosophy* (1863–6) (I, 35) as noted in his 'Philosophy'
Notebook: 'All things must in equity again decline into that
whence they have their origin; for they must give satisfaction

and atonement for injustice, each in the order of time'; 'Definite individual existence constitutes an injustice and must be
atoned for by extinction' (TCD MS10967, 7r).

'fence': partly symbolising Belacqua's state between life and
death, partly reflecting his namesake's position in Dante –
neither on one side nor the other, neither going up nor down.

'casse-poitrine': the active partner in homosexual fellatio; the
word is found among a list of homosexual practices in the *DN*
(481) deriving from Pierre Garnier's *Onanisme seul et à deux*
(1883) (486). Cf. *Dream* (20): 'Casse-poitrinaire'.

'delicious rêverie': possibly derived from Rousseau's *Reveries of a
Solitary Walker* (see *DN* 332 and 333).

'Romeo and Juliet': Cuban cigar named after Shakespeare's play;
the phrase 'smoking his cigar' is included in the list of homosexual practices in *DN* cited above (481).

'to revisit the vomit': 'As a dog returneth to his vomit, so a fool
returneth to his folly' (Proverbs 26:11). In 'Proust' (515), Beckett
connects the vomit with habit: 'Habit is the ballast that chains
the dog to his vomit'; cf. *Waiting for Godot*: 'But habit is a great
deadener' (81).

'exuviae': in a letter to Ruby Cohn (4 January 1982) Beckett suggests 'Exuviae' as a possible title for a miscellaneous volume of
texts, eventually published as *Disjecta* (1983).

'cloud of randy pollen': perhaps by way of Proverbs 16:15, as
noted in *DN*: '(Grateful) as a cloud of the latter rain' (555). Cf.
also the 'cloud of latter rain' in 'A Wet Night' (*MPTK* 48), *Dream*
(200) and the last line of the poem 'it is high time lover'.

'torture chamber, that non-smoking compartment': Beckett is
here recalling his brief stop-over in Nuremberg on his way
from Paris to Kassel in April 1931 to see his cousin Peggy Sinclair; viewing the torture chamber in the castle, Beckett took
note of the no-smoking signs. This experience also finds its
way into *Dream* (71, 181) and the story 'Yellow' (*MPTK* 164, 174),
and is remembered by Beckett on revisiting Nuremberg in

March 1937 ('German Diaries'), and in a letter to Barbara Bray
(2 November 1971).

'Madden prizeman': A prize established in 1798 by Samuel
Madden, awarded to the runner-up in the Trinity College
Dublin Fellowship examination. In Beckett's novel *Watt*
Arsene would have won this prize had he not a boil on
his bottom. A 'maddened prizeman' also appears in the
Addenda to *Watt*.

'picking his nose': taken from Jules Renard's *Journal* entry for 11
September 1893: 'La solitude où l'on peut enfin soigner son nez
avec amour' ('The solitude in which you can at last lovingly pick
your nose'); Beckett annotated the phrase in his personal copy
of Renard and copied it into *DN* (221). Cf. *Dream* (22, 72, 128).

'fiasco': occurs five times in *Dream* (19, 50, 68, 76, 121); Beckett
also used it in a letter to MacGreevy (26 April 1935) with regard
to Octave's impotence in Stendhal's *Armance* (and is used here
to anticipate the 'fiasco' of Lord Gall's impotence). Later in life
Beckett referred to *More Pricks Than Kicks* as a fiasco. Cf. also
the 'occasions of fiasco' that Murphy avoids by escaping to the
'little world' (178), and 'at suck first fiasco' in 'A Piece of Monologue' (265).

'expiation of great strength': possibly derived from William M.
Cooper's *Flagellation and the Flagellants* (1870) (12): 'a dose
of birch of great strength' (*DN* 341). Expiation of original sin
remains an abiding concern in Beckett's work: 'I expiate vilely,
like a pig' (*The Unnamable*).

'hereditaments': property or land that can be inherited; hereditaments are divided into corporeal and incorporeal. A further
nod toward the second part of the story.

'predicateless': from the entry on 'Mysticism' in the *Encyclopedia
Britannica* (14th edn.), noted in *DN*: 'God: predicateless Being,
above all categories' (607). Cf. *Dream* 34.

'triptych': a work of art separated into three sections, usually
applied to panel paintings; in the context of the story, we may

also think of the Holy Trinity and Dante's three-part *Divine
Comedy*.

'begin . . . at the beginning': As the King tells Alice in Lewis Car-
roll's *Alice in Wonderland* (ch. 12), and to 'go on till you come
to the end: then stop'.

'grey shoals of angels': the source of the phrase is unclear, but
has a distinctly Dantean tone, as in *Dream*: 'To do this he had
to liquidate Limbo, he had to eject the grey angels, and dis-
perse with light the shoal of spirits' (63). The 'grey angels' also
appear elsewhere in *Dream* (44).

'womb-tomb': a rhyme used persistently by Beckett.

'smoother than oil and softer than pumpkins': quoting the words
of Ravisius Textor, infamous rector at the University of Paris in
the sixteenth century, on the necessity of whipping the back-
sides of errant boys; taken from Cooper (426) and noted in *DN*
(386). Cf. *Dream* 44.

'grit and glare of his lids on the eyeballs': partly derived from
Renard's *Journal* (24 May 1902), as noted in *DN*: 'Hawk: trembling like an eyelid over a grain of dust' (236); Cf. also *Dream*:
'eyelid over grit' (36), and Beckett's letter to Thomas MacGreevy
(18 October 1932): 'I'm in mourning for the pendu's emission of
semen, what I find in Homer and Dante and Racine and sometimes Rimbaud, the integrity of the eyelids coming down before
the brain knows of grit in the wind' (*LSB I* 134-5).

'looked into his heart': echoes the Muse's admonition in the
opening sonnet of Sir Philip Sidney's sequence *Astrophil and
Stella*: 'Look in thy heart and write'. Underlined in Beckett's
copy of Legouis and Cazamian's *Histoire de la littérature
anglaise* (264).

'soul . . . idly goaded and racked': quoting Augustine (VII, v) (*DN*
128).

'serene yet not relaxedly gay . . . children of joys': the appearance of Zaborovna Privet is based on a long entry in *DN*, in

turn based on Augustine (VIII, xi): 'Continency: serene, yet
not relaxedly gay, honestly alluring me to come, & doubt not;
stretching her [*sic*] forth to embrace me her holy hands full of
multitudes of good examples (grave widows & aged virgins),
not barren, but a fruitful mother of children and joys; smiling
on me with a persuasive mockery' (158). Beckett subverts *Confessions:* if the scene marks St Augustine's conversion, away
from a life of sin, then in 'Echo's Bones' Zaborovna tempts
Belacqua with sexual desire. Zaborovna's entry also echoes the
appearance of Beatrice in Dante's *Divine Comedy.*

'to come and doubt not': as Christ to Thomas, who doubted the
    Resurrection, but here inverted, since it is of course Belacqua
    who is 'resurrected'. Revisited at the end of the story, where
    Belacqua tries to convince Doyle that he is corporeally present.

'anile virgin': Beckett replaces Augustine's 'aged' with 'anile', a
    word which refers to an 'old woman' but also plays on the
    shared etymology of 'anus', indicating that she may not be
    'fruitful'.

'Zaborovna': Zaborovna's occupation of prostitute is inscribed
    in her name, deriving from Russian: 'zabornyj' – 'indecent,
    coarse'; 'zaboristyj anekdot' is a risqué story. As 'zabor' means
    'fence', 'zabornaja literatura' is 'literature of the fence', or por-
    nography; '-ovna' is a possible feminine ending of Russian pat-
    ronymics, thus indicating 'belonging to'. Hence Zaborovna is,
    to an extent, 'of the fence'. Most of Beckett's female characters
    in *Dream* and *MPTK* have names ending with 'a'.

'I don't hear what you say': related to what *Dream* calls an 'aes-
    thetic of inaudibilities', based on Dante's 'chi per lungo silenzio
    parea fioco (hoarse from long silence)' (TCD MS10966/1, 1r).
    Not unlike Virgil in the first canto of the *Inferno*, Zaborovna
    appears as an inaudibility.

'stews': based on Burton (III, 219); cf. *DN*: 'go to the stews or have
    now & then a snatch as they can come by it' (899).

'forty days': Christ spent forty days in the wilderness (Mark 1:13
   and Luke 4:2).

'nuts and balls . . . low stature of animation': from Augustine (I,
   ix), as noted in *DN*: 'He transferred his sins from the rats &
   balls & sparrows of the low stature of childhood' (79); also used
   in *Murphy* (26).

'we is just an impersonal usage, the Tuscan reflexive': The impersonal 'we' as used in academic writing in many languages, to
   avoid the overuse of the passive voice and first person singu-
   lar. Cf. also the narrator in *Dream*: 'we, consensus, here and
   hereafter, of me' (112). 'Tuscan' refers to Dante, born in Flor-
   ence, the capital city of Tuscany, and more specifically to the
   Tuscan dialect used in the *Divine Comedy*.

'mood . . . of self-abuse': 'self-abuse' here as a kind of gram-
   matical masturbation, in that the Tuscan impersonal 'si' can
   be both passive and reflexive (unlike in standard Italian);
   it is thus, in a sense, 'abusing' itself. Cf. 'the alleged joys of
   so-called self-abuse' (*Molloy*, 53 and 54).

'English passive of masochism': plays on the two meanings of
   'passive'; firstly 'submissive', secondly in the passive voice,
   where the subject of a verb refers to the person or thing
   receiving the action described; both of which hint at a kind of
   'masochism'; 'English' in that the passive voice is more commonly used in the English language than in other European
   languages.

'intermissions': not only a narrative device in Beckett's early
   work (including 'Echo's Bones'), but part of a larger aesthetic
   concern with pauses and gaps and silences; cf. for example
   Dream: 'The experience of my reader shall be between the
   phrases, in the silence, communicated by the intervals, not the
   terms, of the statement' (138). The idea is also linked to Marcel
   Proust's 'Les Intermittences du cœur' ('the intermittences of
   the heart'), which was the original title of *À la recherche du
   temps perdu*, and later became the title of an extended passage

of *Sodome et Gomorrhe* ('perhaps the greatest passage Proust ever wrote').

'roaring-meg . . . weary on the way': the sentence is largely taken from Burton (II, 115), where music is 'a roaring-meg against melancholy, a wagon to him that is wearied on the way' (*DN* 802). Cf. *Dream* (38, 85).

'musical . . . thought': relates to Carlyle's *On Heroes, Hero-Worship and the Heroic in History* (291): 'a very musical thought' (*DN* 310). A musical 'pause' follows in the next line.

'sparring for an opening': the first of many phrases based on boxing terminology.

'something between a caress and a dig in the ribs': see also *Murphy*: 'Thus the form of kick was actual, that of caress virtual' (65).

'elevated his mind to God': from an entry in *DN*: 'Quareritur Iº What shall he do who is aware that he is about to experience pollution? R. He shall elevate his mind to God, invoke him, signo cruces se manire, abstain from all voluntary exoneration, renounce the delectation of voluptuousness' (447), from J. B. Bouvier's *Dissertatio in Sextum Decalogi Praeceptum, et Supplementum ad Tractatum de Matrimonio* (1852) (65).

'Dr Keate of Eton': reference to the Eton flagellator Dr Keate, paraphrasing Cooper (438): 'Alas! – said Keate – I cannot guess your name, Boys' bottoms are so very much the same.' Similarly, Belacqua cannot remember Zaborovna's name.

'Privet': Zaborovna's surname is cited for the first time; 'privet' is commonly used to refer to shrubs and small trees of the genus ligustrum, often grown to form a hedge. Taken together with her first name, it confirms her status as a hedge-rambler, or prostitute. Also the Russian informal greeting 'pryvet.'

'shanghaied now': more commonly refers to enforced conscription of men as sailors, but used as here in *Dream* (173).

'number of babies': based on Burton (III, 229): 'looking babies in one another's eyes' (*DN* 907). Cf. *Dream* (19) and 'A Wet Night' (*MPTK* 62).

'old man's desire': cf. 'Softer than an old man's mentula' (John
   Marston, *The Dutch Courtesan*, IV, iii) noted in the 'Whoroscope' Notebook, 'mentula' being Latin for 'penis'.

'absence of any shadow': taken from Dante's *Purgatorio*, where
   Virgil's body has the semblance of a soul and is thus transparent: 'a me nulla s'adombra' ('before me no shadow falls'; III,
   28). In a very early manuscript note on his reading of Dante,
   Beckett wrote 'Dante's shadow, Virgil transparent. Seeing
   only one on ground D. thinks V. gone' (UoR MS4123, 1v). The
   Smeraldina in *Dream* is described as 'casting no shade, herself
   shade' (23).

'spancels': rope or fetter for hobbling cattle and horses, often
   found in Irish folk tales, as well as in W. B. Yeats's *The Celtic
   Twilight*. The word appears in Beckett's notes from Ernest
   Jones's *Papers on Psycho-Analysis* (1912), in which he cross-
   references, in a discussion of the 'Genesis of Symbolism', his
   'Trueborn Jackeen' notes: 'cp. also Trueborn Jackeen and his
   spancels' (TCD MS10971/8, 13r). Cf. also Daniel Corkery's story
   'The Spanceled', published in 1913.

'meatus': meaning 'opening' or 'passage', the word is noted in
   the *DN*, and occurs frequently in Garnier's *Onanisme seul et à
   deux* (476). Cf. *Dream* 157.

'golf tee': a further narrative anticipation, here of Lord Gall.
   Beckett was a passable golfer.

'Wipe them': Taken from J. G. Lockhart's *The History of Napoleon
   Bonaparte* (1829) (470): 'Tears rushed down the cheeks of
   Frederick-William as he fell into the arms of Alexander: "Wipe
   them," said the Czar' (*DN* 56).

'ardent and sad': echoing Baudelaire's definition of beauty in
   Fusées as 'quelque chose d'ardent et de triste'.

'Gilles de Rais' (1404–40), marshal of France, infamous for kid-
   napping and torturing small boys in his pursuit of alchemy
   and necromancy. If there are a 'number of babies' in Zaborovna's eyes, in Belacqua's eyes there is the opposite, Gilles de

Rais's dead children. Beckett will have learnt of de Rais during his reading of Mario Praz's *La carne, la morte e il diavolo nella letteratura romantica* (1930; English tr.: *The Romantic Agony*). His 'orbs' also appear in *Dream* (79).

'strangury': slow, painful urination, evoked by the syntax of this line; the word also appears in 'Ill Seen Ill Said' (81).

'wilful waste': 'brings woeful want', as the proverb has it.

'paps': breasts; *DN* has 'turgent paps' (845), from Burton (III, 89). Cf. *Dream* (50).

'nun of Minsk': a 'sad story' discussed by Cooper in his *Flagellation and Flagellants* and noted by Beckett in *DN* (407); unwilling to renounce Roman Catholicism and convert to the Orthodox Church, the Basilian nuns of Minsk were deported to Siberia in the 1870s and placed in a convent where they were reduced to servants and subjected to floggings.

'cold as January': in Burton, Sophocles was as cold as January (III, 301); changed by Beckett in *DN* to Socrates (968). Cf. *Dream* 61.

'no more capable . . . than Alfieri or Jean-Jacques of dancing a minuet': in his *Autobiography* (mentioned in Beckett's application of 22 July 1932 for a reader's ticket at the British Museum), Vittorio Alfieri admits that he 'abhorred' dancing, a fact exasperated by his dislike of his French dancing master, so that he never knew 'how to dance half a minué' (51); Jean-Jacques Rousseau admitted that despite being 'very well made, I could never learn to dance a minuet', as he was plagued by corns (*Confessions* V).

'drown the babies': from Burton (III, 229). Cf. *DN* (907).

'surface to breathe': in his review of Leishman's translations of Rainer Maria Rilke, Beckett speaks of the German poet 'always popping up for the gulp of disgust to rehabilitate the *Ichgott*' (*Dis* 66).

'clonus': from Greek 'turmoil' or 'tumult', a form of movement marked by alternating contractions and relaxations of a muscle, usually in quick succession. Beckett's poem 'Serena II' refers to 'clonic earth' (*CP* 19).

'happiness, possession of being well deceived': quoting Swift's definition of happiness in his digression on madness in *A Tale of a Tub*, which Beckett had studied at TCD.

'hypnosis': in *DN*, Beckett noted that 'Hypnosis a dominant condition of life' (1154), quoting Jules de Gaultier, 'L'hypnose gouverne tout ce qui est vivant' (*De Kant à Nietzsche*, 1930, 37). Gaultier quotes the myth of 'Titania pressing to her bosom the ass's head of her love' to show the power of desire, hence Beckett's footnote here to 'Titania and the Ass'. Used also in *Dream*: 'pressing à la Titania asses to our boosoms' (160).

'honing': 'longing for'; cf. *DN*, 'don't be honing after home' (818), based on Burton (II, 175): ''Tis a childish humour to hone after home'. In *Dream*, Belacqua hones after the dark (51).

'nervous subject': identified in Beckett's footnote as Shakespeare, *Richard III*, specifically V, iii, where Richard states that 'shadows to-night have struck more terror' to his soul than 'the substance of ten thousand soldiers'.

'motion of the earth . . . system of Galileo': a reference to Galileo's affirmation of the Copernican theory that the earth's movement is controlled by the sun (*Dialogo dei due massimi sistemi del mondo*, 1632). From his reading of James Jeans's *The Universe Around Us* (1929), Beckett noted 'Galileo's investigation of solar system' in *DN* (1041). In *Dream*, the poet Chas declares 'The poem moves, eppure' (324), referring to the phrase 'Eppure si muove' ('Yet it moves'), allegedly muttered by Galileo after he was forced to recant his theory of the earth's movement during an inquisitional hearing in June 1633. Belacqua, standing on the deck of a ship, 'moves forward, like the Cartesian earthball, with the moving ship' (*Dream* 134; repeated in *Molloy* (46) and *The Unnamable* (330). This image may well derive from Beckett's reading of J. P. Mahaffy's *Descartes* (1880): 'The earth did indeed move, but it

was like a passenger on a vessel, who, though he was station-
ary, is nevertheless carried along by the motion of the larger
system which surrounds him' (61). This in turn informed the
'Cartesian' poem 'Whoroscope' (1930), where Galileo appears:
'We're moving he said we're off' and 'That's not moving, that's
moving' (*CP* 40). Cf. also *Watt*: 'and yet it moved, like Galileo's
cradle' (the cradle introduced by way of Arnoldus Geulincx's
Ethics).

'poem by Uhland': unclear which poem Beckett has in mind, but
his knowledge of the romantic poet Ludwig Uhland appears to
have come, as John Pilling discovered, from Heinrich Heine's
essay 'Die Romantische Schule'. Beckett cites this essay, and
alludes to Uhland in his review of Mörike's *Mozart on the Journey to Prague* (*Spectator* 23 May 1934; cf. *Dis* 61–2).

'black cylindrical Galloway cow . . . slipped calf': details in this
passage are taken, mostly verbatim, from Beckett's set of notes
with the heading 'Cow' (TCD MS10971/2, 7v), which note that
to 'slip calf' equals 'abort'.

'greatly eased': as Ruby Tough, having shed her skirt, in 'Love and
Lethe' (*MPTK* 94), and Doyle repeatedly later in this story.

'the article of death': Latin 'in articulo mortis', at the moment of
death.

'don't utter all your mind': Proverbs 29:11 – 'a fool uttereth all his
mind' (*DN* 568).

'mare's-tail': the common name for cirrus clouds.

'Addison's disease': rare condition caused by failure of the adre-
nal glands, resulting, amongst other things, in increased pig-
mentation of the skin.

'pilch': triangular wrapper of cloth, worn over a baby's diaper.

'sail a boat' – echoing the last line of Rimbaud's 'Les poètes de
sept ans': 'et pressentant violemment la voile!' ('and violently
announcing a sail').

'you hedge': in that Zaborovna refuses to answer the question
('When you say "put me up" . . . what do you mean exactly?')

directly, but also playing on her surname. In *Dream*, the Alba's 'immobility' forces Belacqua to 'hedge' (170).

'a crowd': a similar parade of characters occurs during the Fricas' party at the end of *Dream*, in 'What a Misfortune' and 'A Wet Night'. Many of these characters appear in *MPTK*, and their appearance here marks Beckett's attempt to establish narrative consistency between 'Echo's Bones' and the other stories of the collection.

'Vespers . . . Sicilian': Sicilian Vespers is the name given to a bloody uprising on the island of Sicily against French rule in 1282.

'Monthly masquerading as a Quarterly': A swipe at *The Dublin Magazine*, edited by Seumas O'Sullivan. The journal had started out as a monthly, but became a quarterly. *The Dublin Magazine* published Beckett's poem 'Alba' in 1931, but had turned down the poem 'Enueg I' (1931) and, more recently, a short story, possibly 'Ding-Dong' (spring 1933).

'John Jameson o'Lantern': John Jameson, the founder of Jameson's whisky in Dublin, linked to 'Jack O'Lantern', the Irish tradition of carving pumpkins. Mercier and Camier drink 'JJ'.

'exophthalmic goitre': also known as Graves' disease, a form of hyperthyroidism (overproduction of thyroid hormones). Murphy's horoscope cites 'Grave's disease' (21).

'Gipsy Rondo': cf. Haydn's piano trio in G major, nicknamed the 'Gypsy' or 'Gypsy Rondo', because of its Rondo finale in 'Hungarian' style.

'glabrous but fecund': taken from Garnier (485) and noted as 'natura glabrum infecundum' in *DN* (485); from the same source (70) he also noted the word 'glabréité' (smooth-skinned) in *DN* (454). Lord Gall may be bald, but he is not fecund. Cf. the 'glabrous crown' in *Dream* (157) and the 'glabrous cod' in the poem 'To My Daughter' (*CP* 35).

'aguas': from *The Life of Saint Teresa of Avila by herself*; the aguas are the waters with which the contemplative soul is irrigated by God (noted by John Pilling).

'iluminaciones': *Illuminations*, Arthur Rimbaud's collection of
   prose poems, translated into Spanish; cf. 'Staps, the young
   illuminatio' (*DN* 49) taken from Louis Antoine Fauvelet de
   Bourrienne's *Memoirs of Napoleon* (1829–31) (II, 20), and the
   'illuminati' in *Murphy* (107).

'Hairy': Belacqua's best man, 'Hairy' Capper Quin supported
   the Smeraldina after Belacqua's death. Like Lord Gall, he is
   'glabrous', but unlike Lord Gall, his nickname 'Hairy' implies
   potency.

'stiff and open': in *Watt*, the eponymous hero's gait is also 'stiff
   and open' (24).

'Baby Austen': first manufactured in 1922, the Baby Austin was
   a seven-horsepower car for the masses, here conjoined with
   Jane Austen.

'Count of Parabimbi': the Countess of Parabimbi had already
   appeared in *Dream*. The name implies, in Italian, that they are
   'beyond children', i.e. 'without'.

'mending . . . a hard place in Eliot': the phrase is found in *DN*
   (945) with Dante instead of T. S. Eliot; adapted from Burton
   (III, 270).

'to quire their manifesto': quire – 'singing in concert'; Beckett
   ridicules the modernist fascination with publishing manifestos
   (and may be recalling the inclusion of his name by Eugene
   Jolas in the 'Poetry is Vertical' manifesto in *transition*, March
   1932). A quire also refers to a set of twenty-four sheets of paper
   of the same size.

'Poulter's Measure': verse form alternating twelve and fourteen
   syllables, popular in the fifteenth and sixteenth centuries; the
   term derives from poulters' (poulterers') habit of selling sometimes twelve, sometimes fourteen to a dozen.

'thick of the mischief . . . ex-eunuchs': reference to the demise of
   the House of Han as described in H. A. Giles's *The Civilisation
   of China* (1911) (79), and noted in *DN*: 'the eunuchs as usual in
   the thick of the mischief' (518).

'Caleken Frica': mother and daughter Frica appear in *Dream*
and *MPTK*, and are based on Beckett's friend Mary Man-
ning and her mother Susan. 'Caleken' derives from a young
woman called Caleken Peters, held in a corrective institution
run by Cornelius Hadrien, a Franciscan priest who used the
whip to discipline his female penitents – naked, hence the
reference here. Beckett took the story from Cooper (124–33)
and entered her name in *DN* (375). 'Frica' derives from 'fricatrice', as in 'a base harlot, a lewd fricatrice' (Ben Jonson,
Volpone). Beckett found the word in Garnier's *Onanisme seul
et à deux* (448).

'riddle of her navel minnehaha minnehaha': Minnehaha is the
lover of Hiawatha in Henry Wadsworth Longfellow's *The Song
of Hiawatha* (1855). Yet the riddle remains a riddle. 'Hiawatha'
appears in 'Love and Lethe' (*MPTK* 96).

'honeymoon unicorn': in myth, the unicorn could only be sum-
moned and tamed by a virgin; this 'honeymoon' would thus be
another unconsummated affair.

'half-hunter': a watch with a hinged lid; Mr Ash has one in *Watt*,
as does Pozzo in *Waiting for Godot*.

'Yogi': a (traditionally Indian) practitioner of the system of yoga.

'milkman': raw, organic milk is considered to be the most nutri-
tious of foods by yogis.

'standard candle': measurement of light-source intensity, a term
now replaced by the candela.

'leprechaun': spelt variously, the leprechaun is defined as a
pigmy sprite in Irish folklore in the 1817 supplement to O'Reil-
ly's *Irish Dictionary*.

'riding in his brain (abdominal)': reference to the 'abdominal
brain', the solar plexus.

'Debauch and Death': based on an entry in *DN*, 'Debauchery &
Death, Schroud [*sic*] and Alcove' (276), taken from Praz's *The
Romantic Agony* (31), who in turn is quoting Baudelaire's 'Les
deux bonnes sœurs'.

'passed by . . . until the last': copied from Augustine (XI, vi) as
noted in *DN*: 'The non-eternal voice / For that voice passed
by & passed away, began & ended; the syllables sounded &
passed away, the second after the first, the third after the second, and so forth in order, until the last after the rest, & silence
after the last' (189). Cf. also *Dream* (105, 137).

'androgyne': the word 'androgynous' is noted in *DN* (325) and
taken from Praz (206). In *Molloy*, Lousse is described as
'androgyne' (51).

'tempestuous loveliness': quoting Shelley's poem 'On the Medusa
of Leonardo da Vinci in the Florentine Gallery', probably via
Praz (26).

'a spacious nothing': more material from Augustine (VII, i) noted
in *DN* (125): 'A void place, a spacious nothing'. Also used in
Dream (185) and *Murphy* (56).

'Bad one by one . . . very bad all together': Beckett inverts here
a note in *DN* (210) – 'good one by one: very good all together
(Days of Creation)' – based on Augustine (XIII, xxvii).

'rent silk': quoting Giles's *The Civilisation of China* (23), as noted
in *DN*: 'like the melancholy royal Chinese concubine who
loved the sound of rent silk'; the concubine in question is Yang
Kuei-fei (509).

'mandrakes': the mandragora; in common superstition mandrakes grow from the ejaculations of hanged men and scream
when uprooted – hence the 'frightful sound' of the previous
sentence. Cf. *Molloy* (162) and *Waiting for Godot* (9).

'Gnaeni, the pranic bleb': 'Gnani' means 'wise' in several languages. 'Prana', in yoga, is the 'breath' and life principle inhab-
iting all animate things, but here reduced to a 'bleb', a basic
cell organism. 'Prana' reappears in *Murphy* (117).

'A dog . . . the fair': two lines taken from Jonathan Swift's
'Cadenus and Vanessa' (1713), the missing line indicated by the
ellipsis being 'Or some worse brute in human shape'.

'Partagas': a Cuban cigar brand established in 1845.

'Voltigeur': French cigar; Joyce famously won a box of Voltigeurs
  from Sylvia Beach after correctly predicting that George Ber-
  nard Shaw would not subscribe to *Ulysses*.

'hissing vipers of her hair . . . Gorgon': in Greek mythology, Minerva transformed the Gorgon Medusa's beautiful hair into
  snakes, after she was ravished in the temple of Minerva by
  Neptune; Beckett will have come across the story in Ovid's
  Metamorphoses, but the more immediate influence is probably Shelley's poem 'On the Medusa of Leonardo da Vinci in
  the Florentine Gallery' (already quoted earlier in the story) via
  Praz's *The Romantic Agony* (42).

'treed': driven up a tree (or here a fence), as 'a man pursued by
  wild beasts' (*OED*).

'the four and twenty letters . . . diversity of moods': based on
  Burton (I, 408): 'than melancholy conceipts produce diversity
  of symptoms in several persons'. Beckett copied into *DN*: 'the
  four & twenty letters make no more variety of words in divers
  languages than . . . produce variety . . .' (786). Cf. *Dream* 126.

'jigsaw': Beckett to MacGreevy, on the writing of *More Pricks
  Than Kicks*: 'I had been working at the short stories and had
  done about half or two thirds enough when it suddenly dried
  up and I had to leave it there. Perhaps I may get it going again
  now. But it is all jigsaw and I am not interested' (22 June 1933;
  LSB I 168).

'intruding like a flea her loose familiarities into the most retired
  places': from John Donne's 'A Defence of Womens Incon-
  stancy': 'Women are like Flies, which feed among us at our
  Table, or Fleas sucking our very blood, who leave not our most
  retired places free from their familiarity, yet for all their fellowship will they never be tamed nor commanded by us'. Beckett
  also uses the phrase 'admittance to the most retired places' in
  Murphy (30). Cf. also 'Yellow' (*MPTK* 162).

'up hill and down dale': also used in the poem 'Sanies I' (*CP* 12),
  in Beckett's translation of Matías de Bocanegra's poem 'Song

on Beholding an Enlightenment' (*CP* 155) and in *Dream* (72),
where it is linked with the Grimms' tale 'How the Cat and the
Mouse Set Up House'.

'Ninus the Assyrian': from Taylor (I, ii), which tells the story of
Ninus, who had an 'ocean of gold' but 'having mingled his
wines he threw the rest upon the stones'. Once a 'living man',
Ninus is (like Belacqua?) 'nothing but clay'.

'bemired with sins . . . meat of worms': using further material
from Taylor (II, vii): 'Bemired with sins and naked of good
deeds, I, that am the meat of worms, cry vehemently in spirit'.
The line is from a prayer taken from the Euchologion of the
Greek Church for those 'near their death'. Beckett first wrote
'aliment of worms' but replaced it with 'meat of worms', subsequently replacing 'meaty' with 'fruity' in the same line to avoid
repetition.

'agape for the love-feast': the Greek *agape*, in the New Testament,
referred to the 'fatherly love of God for humans, as well as
the human reciprocal love for God. The Church Fathers used
agape to designate both a rite (using bread and wine) and a
meal of fellowship to which the poor were invited' (*Encyclopedia Britannica*). In Latin, the word became synonymous
with 'love-feast'. Beckett's version of the Eucharist (using rum
and garlic) here is rather more sexual than spiritual. In its old
form, 'agape' also means 'gaping', and in this context the word
also relates to the 'horrid jaws'. Beckett uses the word in this
meaning in 'Worstward Ho' (114 and 115). The prose piece 'He is
Barehead' ('Fizzles') has 'hands agape' (224).

'Hutchinson fangs': thick and deeply notched teeth, a result of
hereditary, congenital syphilis. Cf. the 1930s poem 'Spring
Song', which refers to 'the gums the fang of the tongue' (*CP* 46).
Belacqua in 'Dante and the Lobster' has 'fangs' (*MPTK* 13), and
Sucky Moll in *Malone Dies* has a 'solitary fang'.

'bosom pal': cf. 'bosom butty' in *Dream* (49).

'dream of the shadow': another reference to *Dream*.

'sun opened a little eye in the heaven . . . light to a cock': 'But as
   when the sun approaches towards the gates of the morning, he
   first opens a little eye of heaven, and sends away the spirits of
   darkness, and gives light to a cock' (Taylor I, iii).

'lush plush of womby-tomby': cf. Gerard Manley Hopkins's 'The
   Wreck of the Deutschland': 'Warm-laid grave of a womb-life
   grey' (stanza 7) and 'a lush-kept plush-capped sloe' (stanza 8) .

'Elysium': in Greek mythology, the dwelling place of happy souls
   after death.

'guttatim': the word, meaning 'drop by drop', is noted in *DN*:
   'Distillatio (n): semen & mucous – guttatim' (439). Cf. *Dream*:
   'opium guttatim' (86).

'familiar attitude': that is to say embryonic, as Belacqua in Dante.

'spado': a castrated person, a eunuch, or a 'cut and thrust sword'
   (*OED*); cf. 'Draff' (*MPTK* 187).

'tail': refers to the entailment to an estate when a male heir exists.
   This sentence sets up Belacqua's meeting with Lord Gall, who
   is indeed impotent and thus in danger of losing his estate. This
   particular passage is developed in *Murphy*.

'betossed soul': *Romeo and Juliet* (V, iii). Cf. also entry in *DN* (122)
   taken from Augustine: 'The audacious soul – turned it hath &
   turned again, upon back sides & belly – yet all was painful' (VI,
   xvi).

goat: emblematic of the libidinous. In *Murphy*, Miss Carridge has
   a goatish smell, and 'caper[s]' in the 'tragic' mode (82) – the
   word 'tragedy' originally meaning 'goat-song'.

'Jetzer': see *DN* (371): 'Brother Jetzer vomited up the poisoned
   host', taken from Cooper, *Flagellation and Flagellants* (95).
   Johannes Jetzer (1483–1514) was a Dominican lay brother who
   claimed to have had visions of the Virgin Mary. He was subsequently investigated by the Inquisition.

'Juniperus': Appears in *DN* entry (362) listing gymnophists cel-
   ebrating the naked bottom: 'Cynics / Gymnosophists (naked
   sages) / Adamites / Turlupins / Picards / and brother Junipe-

rus'; taken from Cooper (47). Brother Juniperus was a Franciscan monk who emulated Adam's prelapsarian nudity. Cf. *Dream* 98.

'firk': the line 'firked his hide (Rabbinical interpretation of "Gave him of the tree & he did eat")', from Cooper (373; quoting Samuel Butler's *Hudibras*), is in *DN* (380).

'secret love': from Cooper (377): 'Open chastisement is better than secret love' (*DN* 382).

'wearish': cf. the 'little wearish old man (Democritus)' in *DN* (720), used in the poem 'Enueg I' (*CP* 7).

'a little bird': as in superstition; cf. *Murphy* (105).

'that his hour had come': as in John 13:1, referring to the divinely appointed time when Jesus would be glorified through death.

'take it by the forelock': possibly derived from Robert Greene's *Menaphon*: 'Thinking now to . . . take opportunitie by his forelockes'.

'bald': the text as a whole emphasises Lord Gall's baldness, playing on the belief that lack of hair was related to impotence.

'Saint Paul's skull': in Christian art, St Paul is most commonly depicted as bald but with a black beard.

'dundraoghaires': possibly an Irish version of 'dundrearies', long side whiskers worn without a beard. Beckett may also be alluding to the Dublin port of Dun Laoghaire.

'belcher': 'a neckerchief with blue ground, and large white spots having a dark blue spot or eye in the centre, named after a celebrated pugilist called Jim Belcher' (*OED*).

'help to holy living': noted in *DN* (372), taken from Cooper (100). Beckett had also just been reading Taylor.

'Schenectady putter': invented by Mr A. F. Knight of Schenectady, NY, and patented in 1903.

'caoutchouc': India rubber; produced from the resinous juice of certain gum trees, which becomes elastic on exposure to air. Cf. *Dream* 81.

'cap-à-pie': French for 'from head to foot'. Beckett may be alluding to the 'fatherly' attributes of Lord Gall by way of *Hamlet*,
   in which Horatio tells Hamlet that the Ghost was 'A figure like
   your father, / Armed at point exactly, cap-à-pie' (I, ii).
'gutta percha': latex taken exclusively from the Malayan gum
   tree; it differs from caoutchouc, which loses its elasticity when
   cooled.
'tarboosh': 'cap of cloth or felt (almost always red) with a tassel
   (usually of blue silk) attached at the top, worn by Muslims
   either by itself or as part of the turban' (*OED*). Beckett may be
   thinking of Flaubert, who famously wore a tarboosh.
'lost your ball . . . What a shame!': Another reference (via golf
   this time) to Lord Gall's infertility. The words, which provide
   the title of 'What a Misfortune', the seventh story of *MPTK*,
   derive from Voltaire's *Candide* when a eunuch is startled by the
   beauty of Cunégonde: 'O che sciagura d'essere senza coglioni!'
   ('What a misfortune, to be without balls!'). Beckett used the
   phrase in his anonymous satire 'Che Sciagura', which mocked
   the Irish ban on the importation of contraceptives and was
   published in *T.C.D.: A Miscellany* 36 (14 November 1929).
'giant': introduced as a 'colossus', then a 'strange figure', and now
   a fairy-tale 'giant'.
'hundred thousand in a bag': golf balls compensate for Gall's lack
   of potency.
'Lord Gall of Wormwood': wormwood is a bitter shrub that
   sprang up along the writhing track of the serpent driven from
   Paradise; it is commonly associated with gall: 'Remembering
   mine affliction and my misery, the wormwood and the gall'
   (Lamentations 3:19; see also Deuteronomy 29:18). For Burton
   (II, 4), wormwood or Artemisia absinthium is a cure for
   melancholy. It is most commonly seen as an emblem or type
   of what is bitter and grievous to the soul. Cf. Hamlet's 'Wormwood, wormwood' in an aside on hearing the Player-Queen's
   protestations of eternal fidelity to her dying husband, referring

to the bitter taste her promises will produce. Beckett will have come across the name of Gall in Garnier's *Onanisme seul et à deux* (83), as well as Praz's *The Romantic Agony* (146). In the latter, the reference is to the German phrenologist Franz Joseph Gall, as used in *Mercier and Camier* (32). Finally, Beckett is aware of the distinction between 'Gael' and 'Gall', native Irish and foreigner, as used for example in George Sigerson's 1907 book *Bards of the Gael and Gall: Examples of the Poetic Literature of Erin*. Beckett reused the story of Lord Gall as told here in *Murphy* (59), and in *Watt*, the Galls, father and son, are piano tuners, as is their namesake in Joyce's *Ulysses*.

'Possibility of issue is extinct': legal terms of succession; Lord Gall is unable to produce a male heir. Cf. also Beckett's review 'MacGreevy on Yeats', where he mentions 'the issueless predicament of existence' (*Dis* 97).

'The law is a ginnet': more commonly, 'the law is an ass', used in (attrib.) Chapman, *Revenge for Honour* (1634); the substitution here anticipates the discussion of asses and ginnets.

'dream, or rather a vision': another nod towards *Dream*, Rimbaud's 'visionary' poetry and Yeats's *A Vision*.

'could not go on': cf. the closing words of *The Unnamable*: 'you must go on, I can't go on, I'll go on'; also of course Belacqua's attitude in Dante's *Purgatorio*.

'goat': an image of the preterite, those passed over, as in the 'small malevolent goat' of 'Enueg I' (*CP* 7). In the Bible, Christ separates sheep from goats (Matthew 25:32). In *Waiting for Godot*, one of the boys tends goats, the other sheep. There are more goats than sheep in Beckett's work: for example, in *Murphy*, Celia averts her eyes 'like an aborting goat's' (84), while Wylie wonders whether 'a real goat' had been in the house, and in *Watt*, a goat witnesses Mr Hackett falling off the ladder. Goats also appear in 'The Calmative' and *Molloy*.

'Adeodatus': the name of St Augustine's illegitimate son, as noted by Beckett in *DN*: 'Adeodatus (Augustine's bastard)' (175);

based on Augustine (IX, vi), the name appears four times in 'Echo's Bones'. Cf. *Dream*: 'that old bastard of Augustin' (32).

'vexed to the pluck': 'pluck' here in the sense of 'entrails', hence 'annoyed to my innermost being'; Beckett will have found this obsolete usage in Swift's *Journal to Stella*: 'It vexes me to the pluck that I should lose walking this delicious day' (eighteenth letter, 10 March 1710–11).

'quiverfuls': playing on the biblical sense of 'quiverful' as in Psalms 127:5, where it refers explicitly to children: 'Happy is the man that hath his quiver full of them'. Lord Gall's quiver may hold many putters, but he has no offspring.

'edible mushrooms': the appearance of mushrooms in this distorted landscape adds to the fairy-tale aspect.

'When our Lord . . . should go no farther': based on the story of Christ's entry into Jerusalem on Palm Sunday; when the animals refused to carry 'our Lord', he cursed them with sterility. Lord Gall, himself 'sterile', or at least incapable of producing any offspring, praises the ass, who would have done the job 'unconditionally'. In *All That Fall*, Maddy Rooney thinks that Christ rode into Jerusalem on a hinny (a cross between a female ass and a stallion). The issues of sterility in cross-breeding were familiar to Beckett from his reading of Darwin's *Origin of Species* in 1932. At some later point, Beckett noted in his 'Whoroscope' Notebook: 'I think those authors right, who maintain that the ass has a prepotent power over the horse, so that both the mule & the hinny more resemble the ass than the horse; but that the prepotency runs more strongly in the male-ass than in the female, so that the mule, which is the offspring of the male-ass & mare, is more like an ass than is the hinny, which is the offspring of the female-ass & stallion' (80r–81r; loosely quoting Darwin's chapter on 'Hybridism').

'pigdogs': anglicised version of common German term of abuse, 'Schweinehunde'.

'Primo . . . Secun —': in an undated letter to MacGreevy (summer 1929?), Beckett told him that Proust's writing was 'more
heavily symmetrical than Macaulay at his worst, with primos
and secundos echoing to each complacently and reechoing'
(*LSB I* 11). Having finished writing the study *Proust* (published
1931), Beckett thought it was 'not scholarly & primo secundo
enough' to be accepted by publishers Chatto & Windus (letter
to MacGreevy, undated (17 Sept 1930); *LSB I* 48). Cf. *Dream* 51
and 69.

'rosy pudency': cf. Shakespeare's *Cymbeline*, where Imogen is
described as having 'A Pudencie so Rosie' (II, v).

'hog's pudding': a version of the proverbial 'dog's dinner'; possibly based on an entry in *DN* (861), taken from Burton: 'Hungry
dogs eat dirty puddings' (III, 103).

'tenants in tail': legal terminology, describing a situation where
sitting tenants inherit property.

'drownded': obsolete variant spelling of 'drowned'.

'croop': old spelling of 'croup', to 'cry hoarsely' or to 'croak like a
raven, frog, crane' (*OED*).

'bronchi': the two branches of the windpipe.

'pleura': the membrane covering the lung; the word also appears
in *Dream* (139).

'Mazeppa': title of a poem by Byron, in which the eponymous hero
dies after delivering his message; the joke here is presumably
that Belacqua has had to wait for Lord Gall to tell the story.

'translated into Gaelic': a common motif in Beckett's work, used
for example in *All That Fall*. In 'Draff', the example Hairy gives
as being inexpressible in Gaelic is 'O Death where is thy Sting'
(*MPTK* 186). See however an entry in the 'Whoroscope' Notebook: 'a sentence that deserves to be translated into a dead
language' (46r).

'In a vision': thinking of Yeats's *A Vision*.

'impervious to blandishment': cf. note based on Augustine (VII, i)
in *DN*: 'pervious to Thee' (123).

'algum tree': citing II Chronicles 2:8, which refers to the trees
    Solomon used to build the Temple in Jerusalem, and
    appended to a list of words in *DN*: 'analgesia, analgia, analge-
    tic, rectalgia, algum trees out of Lebanon' (1007). Algum trees
    also appear in the poem 'Enueg I', which gave rise to Beckett's
    remark in a letter to MacGreevy: 'Devlin didn't know what an
    algum tree was and I couldn't enlighten him' (9 October 1933;
    LSB I 166).
'Highth': obsolete today, but etymologically more correct, this
    spelling was still used by Milton. Cf. Beckett's letter to MacGreevy
    of 6 November 1955 (*LSB II* 565), in which he quotes Milton's
    'Insuperable height of loftiest shade' (*Paradise Lost* IV, l. 138).
'rub- rather than sud-orem': as noted in *DN*: 'the body roused
    up ad ruborem, non ad sudorem' (799), based on Burton's
    Anatomy of Melancholy: 'till they become flushed', 'not till they
    sweat' (II, 71). Cf. also *Dream* 17–18.
'ad quem': 'limit to which'; in *DN* given as 'terminus a quo & ad
    quem' ('limit from which and to which'; 719). Cf. *Dream* 159
    and 'German Diaries', on walking in the Ohlsdorf cemetery
    'dully without ad quem' (25 October 1936).
'bole': the stem or trunk of a tree.
'vulvate gnarls that Ruskin found more moving than even the
    noblest cisalpine medallions': most probably referring to Rus-
    kin on the painting of trees, which occupies much of volume
    I of *Modern Painters*, disparaging the idealised landscapes of
    both early northern Italian and Classical French painters such
    as Salvator Rosa, Tintoretto, Claude and Poussin – presumably
    the producers of those 'noblest cisalpine medallions' – and
    praising Turner for his rough naturalism. The word 'vulvate' is
    an odd amalgam of obvious words but may well gesture slyly
    towards the legend that Ruskin was unable to consummate his
    marriage to Effie Gray because he was repulsed by either her
    pubic hair or menstrual blood, or indeed both. A reference to
    Modern Painters also appears in *Dream* (16).

'hellebore': type of medical plant often used as a purgative or poison. From Burton (II, 18), Beckett noted: 'Hellebor helps – but not always' (*DN* 793).

'Fräulein Dietrich': Marlene Dietrich; Beckett frequently used the phrase from the song in Josef von Sternberg's *The Blue Angel* (1928), 'sonst, in the words of the song, gar nix' (for example in *Dream* 11 and 17).

'vagitus'; birth-cry, cf. *Murphy* (14 and 44).

'my own, my dear bowels': from Burton (III, 86), as entered in *DN*: 'My own! my dear bowels!' (843); used to address Arland Ussher in a 1934 letter.

'bosses of the buckler': recorded in *DN*: 'I ran against the Lord with my neck, with the thick bosses of my buckler' (133), taken from Augustine (VII, vii).

'rhinal meditation': relating to the nose, in this case Belacqua's desire to pick his nose.

'Sedendo et quiescendo': *DN* (311) has 'sedendo et quiescendo anima efficitur sapiens' ('sitting and meditating the soul grows wise'); this description of Dante's Belacqua is taken from Paget Toynbee's *Dictionary of Proper Names and Notable Matters in the Works of Dante* (1898) (74). Beckett used the phrase as a title for an extract from the unpublished *Dream*, which appeared in *transition*, 21 (March 1932).

'who said that?': based on *DN*, 'Who made all that' (32), taken from Lockhart's *History of Napoleon Bonaparte* (215), quoting Napoleon on 'looking up to the heaven, which was clear and starry'. Cf. 'Who said all that?' in *Dream* (73).

'I came, I sat down, I went away': playing on Caesar's 'I came, I saw, I conquered'; Beckett also used the line in his French essay 'Le Concentrisme' (*Dis* 38).

'quintessence and the upshot': taken from *DN* (790): 'The melancholy man is the cream of human adversity, the quintessence and the upshot', from Burton (I, 434). Cf. *Dream* 77.

'Little wealth, ill health and a life by stealth': variation on Swift's

'Little wealth, and much health, and a life by stealth', from the
    end of Letter XXV in *Journal to Stella*.
'rape': following on from Zaborovna's 'rape' of Belacqua earlier
    in the story. In *DN*, Beckett entered Thomas Aquinas's word for
    rape, 'Stuprum: illicita virginis defloratio' (433).
'oyster on the Aeschylus': Aeschylus, the Athenian dramatist, was
    told by the oracle that he would die by a house collapsing. He
    withdrew to the countryside, but an eagle took his bald head
    to be a stone and dropped a tortoise on him. Beckett took the
    story from Jeremy Taylor's *Holy Dying* (I, i), where an eagle
    drops an oyster (not a tortoise) on Aeschylus. Being bald, Lord
    Gall's skull could easily appear as a stone.
'top-gallant': a nautical term, meaning the head of the topmast
    of a ship.
'Mumm': champagne produced by the house of Mumm in
    Rheims.
'Haemo': meaning 'blood'.
'plethoric': 'suffering from or affected by plethora; having a
    ruddy complexion and a full, fleshy body; excessively full of
    blood, congested' (*OED*).
'collops': a slice of meat; cf. also 'collop-wallop' in *Dream* (1).
'I imprecate the hour I was got': as in Job 3:3: 'Let the day perish
    wherein I was born'.
'scantling of small chat'; the line 'a narrow scantling of language'
    is found in *DN* (196), applied to Augustine's *Confessions*.
'crow's nest': here and elsewhere, the tree house is compared
    with a ship; 'crow's nest' here also anticipates the appearance
    of the submarine.
'Richilda, relict of Albert, Duke of Ebersberg': taken from Taylor
    (I, 2), where the widow Richilda petitions Henry III to restore
    some of her husband's lands to her nephew Welpho; just as
    the king is about to consent, 'the chamber-floor suddenly
    fell under them, and Richilda, falling upon the edge of a
    bathing-vessel, was bruised to death'.

'happy little body': such a 'happy body' also appears in the poem
   'Sanies II' (*CP* 14), in *Dream* (199) and in the short story 'A Wet
   Night' (*MPTK* 47).
'genuine Uccello': Paolo Uccello, Florentine Renaissance painter.
   'Uccello' is Italian for 'bird' – hence a 'genuine' Uccello. The
   reference also adds to the wealth of bird imagery in the story.
   Referring to his application for a post at the National Gallery
   in London, Beckett told MacGreevy: 'Apart from my conoy-
   sership that can just separate Uccello from a handsaw I could
   cork the post as well [as] another' (9 October 1933; *LSB I* 167);
   this in turn is a play on Hamlet's insistence that he knows a
   'hawk from a hand-saw' (II, ii). Beckett also refers to Uccello
   in a 10 May 1934 letter to Nuala Costello, and in the short story
   'Draff' (*MPTK* 182). Cf. also the common slang definition of
   'uccello' as 'penis'.
'O.H.M.S.': On Her/His Majesty's Service.
'grating or triangles': forms of punishment taken from Cooper
   (366), as noted in *DN*: 'Do they tie you to the grating (navy) or
   the triangles?' (379).
'unstuck': as Belacqua had come in 'What a Misfortune', according to the story 'Draff' (184).
'black velvet': beer cocktail of stout (usually Guinness) and
   champagne.
'The jealous swan . . . bode bringeth': ll. 342–3 from Chaucer's *The
   Parlement of Foules*, recorded in *DN* (926); the source here is
   Burton (III, 262).
'supreme abandon': *Dream* opens with a 'supreme adieu', taken
   from Mallarmé's 'Brise marine' ('l'adieu suprême').
'hold in tail male': this means that the entailment upon the
   estate of Wormwood may only be inherited through the male
   line.
'terrestrial Paradises': cf. Dante's *Purgatorio* XXVIII.
'chaplains . . . natural, absolute, perpetual and antecedent': in
   the chapter on 'Impediments in Particular' to marriage, Canon

Law states that 'Antecedent and perpetual impotence to have intercourse, whether on the part of the man or of the woman, which is either absolute or relative, of its very nature invalidates marriage'. In Lord Gall's case, it is 'natural' in that the condition was not brought about by some accident or intervention; 'absolute' in that the impotence manifests itself with any partner; 'antecedent' in that the 'condition' was apparent before the marriage contract; 'perpetual' in that it is incurable. In canonical terms, impotence is 'relative to the concept of consummation'.

'a fruitful earth': from *DN*: 'Onesiphorus, a fruitful earth' (207), based on Augustine (XIII, xxv). Cf. also Psalm 128:3: 'Thy wife shall be as a fruitful vine'.

'priapean': denoting the lascivious or the phallic, the word (often used in the form 'priapic') derives from the Greek god Priapus and his cult. Beckett entered the words 'priapic scenes, priapism' from Praz (198) into *DN* (317). The word also appears in the early poem 'it is high time lover' (*CP* 48).

'Baron Extravas': the name appears in *DN* (478), in notes taken from Garnier (428, 479, 531): 'extra vas, ab ore, parte poste', Latin terms meaning 'outside the vessel', 'by mouth' and 'from behind'. The name suggests that although Extravas has had sexual intercourse with Lord Gall's wife, he has not made her pregnant. See also letter to MacGreevy, 12 December 1932: 'I've been reading a lot of German & trying to write obscene Spencerian stanzas about the Prince of Extravas but I can't do it'.

'protector ... reversioner': Baron Extravas will inherit the Wormwood estate should Lord Gall fail to produce an heir; the estate in that case would be in 'entail'. Lord Gall's dilemma is used, in very similar terms, in *Murphy* (61 and 62).

'fiend in human guise': a 'fiend in human form' appears in Dickens's *Little Dorrit* (ch. 1).

'spirochaeta pallida': syphilis.

'mourning envelope': envelope with black borders, used during a
   period of mourning.
'ashes and dusted a liberal sprinkling of these over his skull': Lord
   Gall's version of the practice, conducted on Ash Wednesday,
   of placing ashes (usually from palm crosses burnt on the previous year's Palm Sunday) on the foreheads of the faithful as a
   sign of repentance. See for example I Maccabees 3:47: 'That day
   they fasted and wore sackcloth; they sprinkled ashes on their
   heads and tore their clothes.'
'maffick': to rejoice wildly; the term derives from the relief of the
   British garrison besieged in Mafeking during the Boer War in
   May 1900 (*OED*); here rather oddly used in conjunction with
   'grief.'
'Disentail': to break or cut off the entail of the estate whereby its
   succession is determined.
'double-fisted attack on his breasts': cf. entry from Ovid, *Metamorphoses* (III, l. 481) in *DN* (1116): 'nudaque marmoreis per-
   cussit pectora palmis' ('He beat his bare bosoms with marble
   palms). Cf. also *Dream* 227 and 'A Wet Night' (*MPTK* 73).
'peppered': infected with venereal disease.
'blobbers': thick or protruding lips; Sucky Moll in *Malone Dies*
   has a 'blobber-lip', concealing her syphilitic 'solitary fang.'
'sine qua non': Latin for 'without which not'; refers to an essential
   condition, element or consequence.
'considering cap': Ignatius Gallaher uses such a cap in Joyce's
   story 'A Little Cloud' (in *Dubliners*), 'when he was in a tight
   corner'; Belacqua also wears one in *Dream* (63).
'Lord Doyle': presumably Beckett's error, anticipating the intro-
   duction of the character Doyle in the third part of the story.
   However, names are interchangeable in this text – see for
   example the very next line.
'Baron Abore . . . Partepost': Latin for 'by mouth' and 'from
   behind', the two terms deriving from the entry in *DN*, 'extra vas,
   ab ore, parte poste' (478), taken from Garnier (428, 479, 531).

All of these terms denote sexual activities that do not lead to
conception; the following passage contains several references
to homosexuality.

'I have it': words also uttered by Celia in *Murphy*, having picked
up Murphy's horoscope. Murphy however, with the response
'Don't I know', thinks she is referring to the pox.

'Hair!': a poor joke, as Lord Gall has neither 'hair' nor an 'heir'.

'chaps': jaws or cheeks.

'impubescence': that is to say, prepubescence; absence of hair is
throughout the story linked with infertility.

'perish the day!': cf. Job: 'Let the day perish wherein I was born'
(3:3).

'bald as a coot': proverbial, and cf. Burton (III, iii) – coots are
water birds whose heads appear to be bald.

'It is time I was getting on': taken from *Dream* (195).

'Frascatorian': Beckett is thinking of Girolamo Fracastoro (1478–
1553), Italian physician and poet famous for his *Syphilis sive
morbus gallicus* (*Syphilis or The French Disease*). Cf. also letter
to MacGreevy (6 February 1936): 'Translate Fracastoro's Sifil-
ide e poi mori' (*LSB I* 314), a reference to the famous line 'vedi
Napoli e poi muori' (see Naples and die).

'eversore': Beckett noted 'Carthaginian Eversores' in *DN* (86). He
took the word from Augustine's *Confessions*, where 'eversores'
refers to the 'overturners' who aimed to overthrow Carthage;
Baron Extravas similarly aims to 'ruin' Lord Gall.

'squared up ... gamecock': boxing imagery.

'dauntless': an entry in *DN*, taken from Lockhart's *The History of
Napoleon Bonaparte* (552), reads: 'Did he humbug you Hinton,
dauntless boatswain' (66). Elsewhere in Beckett's early work,
the word is linked with Dean Inge's description 'St Teresa:
undaunted daughter of desires' (*DN* 695); in *Dream*, the Alba
is the 'dauntless daughter of desires' (222), also in 'A Wet Night'
(*MPTK* 68), and the poem 'Sanies I' refers to the 'dauntless
nautch-girl on the face of the waters'.

'aspermatic': lacking, or unable to ejaculate, semen; the words 'dry priapism, aspermatisme' are found in *DN* (470), taken from Garnier (280). Cf. also Beckett's reference to 'months of aspermatic nights & days' in a letter to MacGreevy (12 September 1931; *LSB I* 87). In his 'German Diaries', Beckett noted the fact that during a lecture on Proust, Professor Brulez cited Huxley's 'intellectual masturbation' (*Eyeless in Gaza*), and responded in his diary: 'Better at least than mental aspermatism' (19 November 1936).

'my position': Belacqua's foetal position in Dante's *Divine Comedy* and in Beckett's *Dream* (227).

'Stand up . . . little soldier': another poor joke, as Lord Gall's little soldier does not, metaphorically speaking, stand up. Already in 'Yellow', Belacqua 'must efface himself altogether and do the little soldier' (*MPTK* 163).

'zebra . . . act on the brainwave': taken from Renard's *Journal* (27 January 1905) as noted in *DN*: 'rapid as a zebra's thought' (239); thus Lord Gall is thinking 'rapidly'. Also used in *Dream* (184) and *Murphy* (27).

'Wine is a mocker': citing Proverbs 20:1: 'Wine is a mocker, strong drink is raging: and whosoever is deceived thereby is not wise'.

'tilly dawson': a night-cap.

'barmaid . . . bit her': the joke reappears in *Murphy* ('Why did the barmaid champagne? . . . Because the stout porter bitter', 85) and subsequently in *Watt* (with the whiskey 'Power').

'facile, sweet and plain': citing Taylor (III, 2), with the preceding words being 'The work of our soul is cut short', but with a nod toward Dante's 'dolce stil novo' (sweet new style), used in 'Ding Dong' (41) and the poem 'Home Olga' ('sweet noo style').

'distinct . . . extinct': the issue of the discussion may be 'distinct', but the issue in terms of an 'heir' is extinct.

'borne up on the way down': referring to Luke 4:9-14, as Satan suggests that Jesus cast himself from the Temple trusting that he will be 'borne up' by angels.

'yoke . . . lightly': citing Matthew 11:30: 'my yoke is easy, and my
   burden is light'.

'wring your withers': stir the emotions or sensibilities; cf. *Hamlet*:
   'let the galled jade wince, our withers are unwrung' (III, ii). Cf.
   also 'A Wet Night' (*MPTK* 51).

'husbandlike': Lord Gall may be capable of husbandry, but not of
   acting like a husband.

'keep up your pecker': colloquial, in terms of remaining cheerful
   or steadfast, but with a sexual pun.

'Emptybreeks': as Liam O'Flaherty states in *The Black Soul* (1928),
   'the deadliest insult', since being 'childless was to be impotent'.

'afternoon had . . . worn away': as in Dickens, *The Old Curiosity
   Shop* (ch. 26).

'quinquina': French name for a South American aperitif introduced to Europe by Spanish missionaries in the seventeenth
   century. Also anticipating the appearance of Capper 'Hairy'
   Quin.

'anxious to be gone': in *Krapp's Last Tape*, Krapp is 'burning to be
   gone' (10).

'quomodo': the manner, or means by which to get going.

'Moby Dick of a miracle': in *DN*, Beckett noted the expression
   'Whale of a miracle' (209), taken from Augustine (XIII, xxvii)
   and used in *Dream* (181). Here the quote is coupled with Melville's novel, which Beckett had read since writing *Dream* (letter to MacGreevy, 4 August 1932).

'forrader': colloquial or dialect form of 'forwarder', of being further forward.

'Don't rip up old stories': don't repeat yourself; as an entry in
   the 'Whoroscope' Notebook indicates, Beckett took this from
   Henry Fielding's *Tom Jones* (IX, vi). Cf. also *Murphy* (11).

'image . . . shadow': the correlation is set up in the myth of the
   cave in Plato's *The Republic*.

'precluded from looking into my eyes': Belacqua's narcissistic
   habits are denied.

'Shuah': Beckett took Belacqua's surname from Garnier (16), as
    an entry in *DN* reveals: 'Er, Onan and Shelah, sons of Judah &
    Shuah' (425); as Genesis 46:12 states, Shuah is the mother of
    Onan.
'bottle and a mirror': Burton – 'spending her time between a
    comb & a glass' (quoted *DN* 858). Cf. also *Dream* (50).
'old itch': *DN* (443) contains an entry – 'prurience, prurigo, prurit'
    – from Garnier (24, 35, 131), all referring to 'itching'; cf. *Dream*
    (19, 56, 108, 181), the 'rationalist prurit' in *Murphy* (115) and
    Mr Nackybal's 'diffuse ano-scrotal prurit' in *Watt*. Complaining
    about requests by publishers to cut passages from *Murphy*, he
    told MacGreevy that his next work would fit on sheets of toilet
    paper, and 'also in Braille for anal pruritics' (*LSB I* 383).
'mirror . . . wipe my face off it': from Renard's *Journal* (18 Febru-
    ary 1892); marked in Beckett's personal copy and noted in *DN*
    (218): 'Quand il se regardait dans une glace, il était toujours
    tenté de l'essuyer' ('when he saw himself in the looking-glass,
    he always tried to wipe it'). Also used in *Dream* (22, 47, 128).
    Like Narcissus, Belacqua consistently sees his own image in a
    mirror.
'continent . . . sustenant': drawing on *DN*: 'The 2 virtues: to con-
    tain (oneself from so-called goods of this world); to sustain
    (the evils of the world)' (183), summarising a passage in Augus-
    tine (X). Cf. also *Dream* (46, 73).
'titter affliction out of existence': a version of the *risus purus*, the
    laugh of laughs about unhappiness in *Watt* (39), and cf. 'Noth-
    ing is funnier than unhappiness' in *Endgame* (26).
'Christian . . . bleeding science': Belacqua's assumption of Augus-
    tinian ideas is rapidly dismissed by Lord Gall. Members of the
    Christian Science Church, founded in the late nineteenth cen-
    tury, rely on prayer to God for healing rather than medicines or
    surgery; as such they normally refuse blood transfusions.
'steps . . . drew them up': Beckett is here referring to the well-
    known image of the ladder of knowledge, first used by the

Ancient Greek sceptic Sextus Empiricus in *Against the Logi-cians*; Beckett rediscovered the idea in his reading of Fritz Mauthner and Ludwig Wittgenstein, who use it to discuss what language cannot convey.

'Magna Graecia': 'Great Greece' of antiquity, and by extension ancient philosophy; a hand-drawn map of 'Magna Graecia' can be found at the beginning of Beckett's 'Philosophy' Note-book' (TCD MS10967).

'apex of neutrality': possibly inspired by W. R. Inge's *Christian Mysticism* (7), as an entry in *DN* suggests: 'apex of the mind' (676), St Bonaventura's *apex mentis*.

'Socrates . . . white-headed': cf. *DN*, 'Socrates was as cold as Janu-ary' (968), taken from Burton (III, 301) but replacing Sophocles with Socrates (as in *Dream* 61). Cf. also Lennox Robinson's popular Irish comedy *The Whiteheaded Boy* (1916).

'delicious irony . . . turned up the tail of his abolla': the abolla was a garment in ancient Roman times worn by peasants, soldiers, and by philosophers 'as an affectation' (*OED*). The reference here is to Socrates, on trial for his life, lifting the tail of his abolla in order to observe the call of nature (and thus exposing his buttocks). Hence the 'delicious irony'. The line is repro-duced in *Murphy* (120).

'walls, happily padded': as are the cells in the Magdalen Mental Mercyseat in *Murphy* (101, 109).

'aerie': the nest of a bird of prey, or more generally the nest of any large bird, esp. one that nests high on cliffs or tall trees. Mur-phy's garret is described as an 'aery' (99).

'aerie . . . children': the proximity of these two words may suggest that Beckett was thinking of the 'aery of children' in *Hamlet* (II, ii).

'Bide a wee': the affected tone of the previous exchange slips into dialect, as Lord Gall uses a Scottish accent (Belacqua retaliates with Middle English).

'I mot gon hoom . . . the sonne draweth weste': Chaucer, *Leg-end of Good Women* (l. 153, B text in Skeat's edition). Beckett

had copied it, together with the beginning of the subsequent
line 'To Paradys . . .' in *DN* (1176); the reference to 'Paradys' is
tellingly omitted: Lord Gall's view of Wormwood as a 'terrestrial Paradise' is not shared by Belacqua. This anticipates the
coming of dawn later in the story, before which the 'ghost'
Belacqua must be gone, as must Hamlet.

'green as Circe's honey': the line 'Green honey of Circe' is in
DN (710), and derives from Homer, *Odyssey* (X, 166). This is
Beckett's version of 'miel vert', as he read the book in Bérard's
French translation (cf. letter to MacGreevy, September 1931).
Cf. also *Dream* 155.

'asphodel': most likely with the symbolism it carries in *Odyssey*
(XI, 539): a flower made immortal by poets, and said to cover
the Elysian fields, according to Greek myth and religion.

'An ego jam sedeo?': 'am I now sat?'; the line is said to be Sene-
ca's regarding the rich fool who was lifted from his baths
onto a soft couch, but Beckett presumably took it from Taylor
(I, iii).

'Latin flogged into us at school': when asked about the origin
of his Latin proficiency, Johnson answered 'My master whipt
me very well' (Boswell, *Life of Samuel Johnson*; noted by Seán
Lawlor).

'woolpack': popular name for 'fleecy' cumulus clouds (*OED*).

'Archipelagoes . . . glades': echoing ll. 83–4 of Rimbaud's poem
'Le Bateau ivre', which Beckett translated ('Drunken Boat')
in early 1932: 'I saw archipelagoes of stars and islands
launched me / Aloft on the deep delirium of their skies'
(*CP* 66).

'pollards': trees that have their upper trunks and branches cut
back to give them uniform shape; 'bald-headed' (obsolete).

'Cut out the style': referring to Belacqua's imitation of Rimbaud's
style (in particular the use of plurals).

'young person, paddling in the moat': cf. last line of Rimbaud
'Les poètes de sept ans'.

'a sweet column of quiet': from Burton (III, 249), referring to a 'good wife', as indicated by the note in *DN*: 'a column of quiet (a good wife)' (916). Cf. *Dream* 23.

'partner of my porridge days': entered in *DN* (542) and deriving from Giles's *The Civilisation of China* (192), in which it refers to Sung Hung's loyalty to his wife with whom he has endured poverty. Cf. *Dream* (183).

'vieux jeu': literally 'old game', meaning old-fashioned.

'champaign land': from Alphonse de Lamartine's *Méditations poétiques*, and used variously by Beckett in *Dream* (9 and 43), 'Fingal' and 'Walking Out' (*MPTK* 24 and 103), the poem 'Enueg I' (*CP* 6), and *Mercier and Camier* (77).

'diadems': crowns, adornments.

'crocodile': colloquial term for children walking two and two in a long row. This is the second appearance of a parade of characters new and old.

'Festooned': presumably Smeraldina is pregnant with Hairy Quin's babies, as it was Hairy who proposed to replace Belacqua in her affections in 'Draff'. There is a 'festoon of words' in *Dream* (226) and in 'A Wet Night' (*MPTK* 72).

'cynic in a spasm': an entry in *DN* reads 'cynic spasm [?]' (477), and is taken from Garnier (409ff); according to Garnier, these are convulsions produced by masturbating with objects.

'Nazi with his head in a clamp': Beckett is remembering his visit to the torture chamber in the castle at Nuremberg in April 1931, and assimilating this to the fact that the city was an early stronghold of the Nazi party, from September 1933 onwards.

'monster shaped like mankind exactly': a parody of the act of the Christian God or Prometheus forming mankind in their image, with a nod toward Mary Shelley's *Frankenstein* and Goethe's poem 'Prometheus'.

'Dáib and Seanacán': Gaelicised versions of David and Jonathan (Book of Samuel). Their names appear in a list of classical

models of male friendship in Burton (III, 28); Beckett entered
some of these into *DN* (813): 'Damon & Pythias', 'Pylades &
Orestes' (used in 'Ding-Dong'; *MPTK* 37), 'Nisus & Euryalus'
and 'Theseus & Pirithous'. David and Jonathan are very close
friends, as indicated by the reference to the 'four legs in three
tights and half a codpiece', and the fact that they are 'related'
when they are next mentioned.

'passed by and passed away': copied from Augustine (XI, vi) as
noted in *DN*: 'The non-eternal voice / For that voice passed
by & passed away, began & ended; the syllables sounded &
passed away, the second after the first, the third after the second, and so forth in order, until the last after the rest, & silence
after the last' (189).

'pram I found most moving': cf. the scene in Sergei Eisenstein's
film *Battleship Potemkin*, in which a pram slowly rolls (moves)
down the Odessa steps. Beckett would write a letter to Eisenstein in 1936 asking whether he could join his film institute in
Moscow.

'utile dulci': from Horace, *Ars Poetica* (l. 343); quoted by Burton
on the frontispiece of *The Anatomy of Melancholy*: 'Omne tulit
punctum qui miscuit utile dulci, lectorem delectando pariter-
que monendo' ('He that joins instruction with delight, profit
with pleasure, carries all the votes').

'cutwater': placed at the head of a ship, the cutwater divides the
water before it reaches the bow; associated with the Frica's
breasts in *Dream* (215), and the corresponding passage in 'A
Wet Night' (*MPTK* 61).

'Night fell like a lid': as it does toward the end of the first act in
Waiting for Godot – '*In a moment it is night*' (43).

'the fare': in *Dream* (211) the burden of paying the Jesuit's tram
fare falls to the Polar Bear.

'conductor': the conductor in *Dream* (158) is both slow and Irish.

'the bone is still there': an allusion to the title of the story, 'Echo's
Bones'.

'Only time (if and when he eats it)': from the Latin 'tempus edax,' the idea of time as 'devourer of all things' found for example in Ovid, *Metamorphoses* (XV, l. 234). The Latin tag appears in 'Walking Out' (*MPTK* 113).

'Now to move the limbs of the body . . . now not': noted in *DN* (143) and based on Augustine (VII, xix).

'divide, multiply . . . mind by thinking': the act of distinguishing images of the essential soul from phantasms; also taken from Augustine (VII, xvii) and noted in *DN* (141).

'Mary nor Martha': in the Bible, Mary and her sister, the servant Martha, are emblems of contemplative and active lives, respectively (John 11:1). Moran's servant in *Molloy* is also called Martha.

'bubble me': expression taken from Henry Fielding's *Tom Jones* (XII; VII), and entered in the 'For Interpolation' section of the 'Whoroscope' Notebook, kept toward the writing of *Murphy*.

'In fine': Latin 'in the end.'

'humblecumdumble': the word, meaning 'humble servant,' appears in Letter 10 of Swift's *Journal to Stella*. Beckett used the word to sign off letters to Arland Ussher (1934) and Jocelyn Herbert (16 June 1966).

'Death . . . improved': cf. 'Draff,' Hairy Quin 'was greatly improved'; his 'face improved rapidly' (*MPTK* 180).

'incorruptible . . . uninjurable . . . changeability is of the narrowest': *DN* contains the note 'incorruptible, uninjurable & unchangeable' (124), from Augustine (VII, i). Beckett quotes it, unchanged, in *Dream* (41). The word 'incorruptible' appears in the essay 'Recent Irish Poetry' (*Dis* 70), the poem 'Malacoda' and *Murphy* (118). The guard in 'A Wet Night' has an 'incorruptible heart' (*MPTK* 72). Cf. also I Corinthians 15:52: 'and the dead shall be raised incorruptible.'

'after the manner of all the earth': quoting Genesis (19:31), where the daughters of Lot seek to lie with their father.

'toe the scratch': colloquial; to be ready and willing.

'call his name Haemo': echoes the angel Gabriel's words when announcing to Mary that she will conceive, and will 'call his name Jesus' (Luke 1:28-31).

'puddle of iniquity': a note in *DN* (889) reads 'more envious than the pox (porky quean) & within a puddle of iniquity', and is taken from Burton (III, 205).

'me made a father': quoting Burton (III, 104), 'She made me a father', and noted in *DN* (862). Cf. *Dream* (117).

'Shameful spewing': More Burton (II, 246) from *DN* (821): 'Woe be to him that makes his neighbour drunk: shameful spewing shall be upon his glory'. Cf. also *Dream* (123) and the poem 'Home Olga'.

'clubbed index': Beckett has another 'index' in mind here, as an entry in *DN* (472) shows: 'clubbed penis of the exclusive masturbator', from Garnier (288). The subtext here is that Gall masturbates excessively and 'exclusively', something that in popular belief causes infertility.

'vestryman': cf. *Dream* (79) and the 1929 poem 'Return to the Vestry' (*CP* 245).

'Moll': common name for prostitute, and she is also syphilitic; cf. *DN* entry 'syphilis; toga virilis' (486), amended in a letter to MacGreevy of 8 October 1932 to 'toga mollis'. Moll is also the name of Macmann's lover in Beckett's novel *Malone Dies*.

'Olympian': the word is recorded in Rachel Burrows's notes from Beckett's TCD lecture on Corneille. Belacqua has 'Olympian fancies' in 'What a Misfortune' (*MPTK* 116).

'die . . . intestate': to die without having made a valid will, so that the estate comes under the rules of inheritance. In the absence of an heir, Lord Gall's estate would revert to Baron Extravas.

'Picking at the bed-clothes': a medical symptom indicating the approach of death.

'Hungry dogs eat dirty puddings': taken verbatim from Burton
    (III, 103; footnote), and entered in *DN* (861).

'more God in an elephant than in an oyster': based on Augus-
    tine (VII, i); in *DN* this reads: 'More God in an elephant than
    in a sparrow (Sophistry of spatial divinity)' (126). Lord Gall's
    response can be related to another passage from the *Confes-
    sions* (III, 7) recorded in *DN*: 'God's being not bulk; for the
    infinite bulk contains parts lesser than its infinitude; so not
    wholly everywhere' (87).

'Oh les femmes et les framboises': quite possibly the chanson
    'Les fraises et les framboises', adapted by Serge Claude with
    music by E. Wolff.

'non-spatial divinity': from Augustine (VII, i); in *DN* this reads:
    'More God in an elephant than in a sparrow (Sophistry of
    spatial divinity)' (126).

'centre your notes like a lepidopterist': as lepidopterists display
    butterflies and moths.

'seamstress': the word appears in *DN* (474) and is taken from Gar-
    nier's *Onanisme seul et à deux* (448):

> the breastless } frixatrix (seamstress)
> sabre-flat }

Beckett may be referring here to 'invisible mending', repairing
cloth by taking and then reweaving individual threads of the
same type from concealed parts of the garment.

'Père, Fils and Saint Esprit': French for Father, Son and the Holy
    Ghost.

'out of Pernod': Pernod Fils was a popular brand of absinthe
    before it was banned in 1915. One of its ingredients was worm-
    wood, and when drunk excessively it caused impotence.

'Fernet Branca': a very strong liqueur, which is also drunk in
    Dream (37).

'Ach Kinder!': German for 'Oh Children!'

'a few oysters': because they have aphrodisiac qualities; the
    phrase 'oyster kiss' is entered in *DN* (922) from Burton (III,
    256), and used in *Dream* (17), 'Le Concentrisme' (*Dis* 39) and
    Murphy (71).

'oysters . . . too succulent': Cf. entry in *DN*, 'succulent bivalve' (639),
    possibly deriving from the 'Circe' chapter of Joyce's *Ulysses*.

'prehended the bole': i.e. grasped or seized the trunk of the tree.

'cataclasm': a violent breakdown or disruption.

'omnia vincit': Latin for 'conquers all'; a subversion of the Wife of
    Bath's 'amor vincit omnia' in Chaucer's *Canterbury Tales*, as in
    'Text 3': 'Niño, you need a shave, / but Vaseline omnia vincit'
    (*CP* 38).

'exanthem': anglicised form of 'exanthema', a rash. Borrowed,
    with subsequent phrasing, from *Dream* (82).

'tree trunk yawn': common motif in fairy tales and children's books.

'ostrich': cf. the 'peacostrich' in the poem 'Spring Song'. The
    ostrich is a version of Geryon, the griffin that carries Dante
    and Virgil in Purgatory.

'Strauss . . . simply waltzes': Beckett is punning on the German
    word for ostrich, 'Strauss', and the composers of waltzes,
    Johann Strauss the Elder and Johann Strauss the Younger.

'care to pry into mysteries . . . great enterprise': because Belacqua
    had just stated 'I never care to look into motive'. The grounds-
    man in 'Draff' also 'lost interest in all the shabby mysteries'
    (*MPTK* 174).

'she DOES': responding to the implied question (asked also in
    Dream, 223), 'Does she do it?'; in the typescript, Beckett origi-
    nally wrote 'does she –' before replacing it with 'would she –'.

'mollified': an entry in DN (449) reads: 'molles (effeminate) St.
    Paul'; this is taken from the New Testament in Latin, I Corinthi-
    ans 6:9, and also appears in Burton's *Anatomy of Melancholy*
    (II, 146). This note thus links 'Moll' with 'Gall' through St Paul's
    baldness. Lousse tries to 'mollify Molloy' in *Molloy* (42).

'galling': is to Gall what 'mollified' is to 'Moll.'

'Diana's well': taken from Burton (III, 285–6): 'Diana's well, in
which maids did swim, whores were drowned' (DN 962). As
Lady Gall has contracted syphilis from Baron Extravas, the
answer does not surprise. Also used in *Dream* (34).

'to go in unto': biblical formulation; given Belacqua's surname, Beckett may specifically be thinking of the story in
Genesis 38:2–4: 'And Judah saw there a daughter of a certain
Canaanite, whose name was Shuah, and he took her, and
went in unto her. And she conceived, and bare a son; and
he called his name Er. And she conceived again, and bare
a son; and she called his name Onan.' Cf. also Genesis 16:2,
as it relates to infertility. 'And Sarai said unto Abram, Behold
now, the Lord hath restrained me from bearing: I pray thee,
go in unto my maid; it may be that I may obtain children by
her.'

'puella': Burton (III, 238) furnished Beckett with the following
note in *DN* (913): 'a lascivious & petulant virgin puella.' Winnie
in the story 'Fingal' is a 'quiet puella' (*MPTK* 26).

'clitoridian': the word is noted in *DN* (456) – 'clitoridian (exu-
berance)' and derives from Garnier's *Onanisme seul et à deux*
(78–9); cf. 'clitoridian puella' in *Dream* (111), a letter to A. J.
Leventhal (26 July 1934) and a letter to Thomas MacGreevy
(8 September 1935), in which he describes Nuala Costello as
'unclitoridian' (*LSB I* 274).

'cacoethes': uncontrollable urge or 'itch'; most famously used
in Juvenal's seventh satire as the itch to write, as noted in *DN*
(1018): 'cacoethes (scribendi, loquendi).' The 'Whoroscope'
Notebook gives 'tenet insanabile multos scribendi cacoethes'
(84r). Used in *Dream* (133) with regard to Joyce. The word
'kakoethes' appears in the deleted opening of the poem 'Serena I' (*CP* 284).

'wild civility': Robert Herrick praises a 'wild civility' in his poem
'Delight in Disorder.'

'ripping . . . topping': archaic public-school slang for 'splendid' or 'excellent'; both words carry sexual double entendres.

'lapped': at the beginning of the story, Belacqua's eyeballs are 'lapped in gloom'.

'Lethe': in Greek mythology a river in Hades, the waters of which induce forgetfulness.

'uterotaph': a version of one of Beckett's favourite words, 'womb-tomb', combining here the Latin and the Greek roots respectively.

'essentially a girl': which leaves Lord Gall without an heir.

'So it goes in the world': these are the words that conclude the story 'Draff', and thus *MPTK* as it was published. The phrase is taken from the Brothers Grimm story 'How the Cat and the Mouse Set Up House'; Beckett quoted the German original in a letter to George Reavey (26 May 1938) and in the letter dated 20 August 1970 in which he told Kay Boyle that he had 'capitulated' to requests to have *MPTK* reprinted. Beckett's shorthand for a weary acceptance of the ways of the world, it is also found in letters to Pamela Mitchell (7? January 1955) and Barbara Bray (23 August 1967 and 27 May 1977).

'see above, page 7, paragraph 2': that is, back on the fence, after his adventure with Zaborovna.

'total extinction': in a letter to MacGreevy (4 August 1937), Beckett stated that Samuel Johnson had been in 'horror at ultimate annihilation, to which he declared in the fear of his death that he would prefer an eternity of torment' (*LSB I* 529).

'R.I.P.': 'Requiescat in Pace'; before inserting this 'rest in peace', Beckett on the typescript had originally written 'inscription, which had no literary value'. In 'Draff', Hairy Quin tells the Smeraldina that Belacqua had once told him an inscription 'he would have endorsed, but I can't recall it' (*MPTK* 190). Beckett's interest in headstone inscription is epitomised by the narrator in 'First Love', whose epitaph 'meets with my approval' more than any of his 'other writings': 'Hereunder lies the above who up below / So hourly died that he lived on till now' (26).

'sea': the fact that the graveyard is by the sea brings to mind Paul
     Valéry's poem 'The Graveyard by the Sea', as well as Greystones
     cemetery, where Beckett's father is buried.
'Attic': pertaining to Attica or its capital Athens, with connota-
     tions of classicism and elegance.
'classico-romantic': this whole passage is a pastiche of Romantic
     and Homeric material, and was transferred to the end of the
     story 'Draff' after 'Echo's Bones' had been rejected by Chatto &
     Windus. The antithetical play between 'romantic' and 'classi-
     cal' is taken, nearly verbatim, from the opening paragraphs of
     Mario Praz's *The Romantic Agony*.
'words of the rose to the rose: "No gardener has died, within
     rosaceous memory."': The source is given in *DN* (581): 'R.
     de d'A. Ephemeral sophism. Fontanelles [*sic*] rose that
     said no gardener had died within the memory of roses . . .'
     From Bernard de Fontenelle, *Entretiens sur la pluralité des
     mondes* (1686), but taken by Beckett from Diderot, *Le Rêve de
     d'Alembert* (1769). Cf. also *Dream* (175) and 'Draff' (191), where
     the 'rose' is the nozzle of the gardener's hose. Beckett cited the
     line in a letter to Avigdor Arikha dated 14 January 1977, adding
     that the 'conceit' is in Fontenelle.
'a little song': adapting Léo Daniderff's comical song *Je cherche
     après Titine* (1917), later made more famous when Chaplin
     sang a garbled version of it in *Modern Times* (1936). Beckett
     replaces 'I'm looking for you, Titine' with 'I love you': 'I love
     you, Titine / I must love you forever / Because you are the
     raisin / In the cake of my life'. The groundsman (Doyle) sings a
     little song at the end of 'Draff' (*MPTK* 191).
'submarine of souls': echoing Charon's ferry carrying souls across
     the river Styx and into Hades in Greek mythology. Cf. also
     Belacqua's funeral in 'Draff', 'All aboard. All souls at half-mast.
     Aye-aye' (*MPTK* 185), and the poem 'Malacoda': 'All aboard all
     souls / half-mast aye aye' (*CP* 21).

'Alba': Belacqua is not the only familiar character in this
   post-mortem world; Alba Perdue, based on Beckett's love
   interest Ethna MacCarthy, is one of the main female characters
   in *Dream* and *MPTK*. In 'Draft', we are told that the Alba died
   'in the natural course of being seen home' (*MPTK* 175).

'flamingo': in the poem 'Sanies I', the 'old black and flamingo'
   relates to Ethna MacCarthy's attire.

'One hundred and fiftythree iridiscent fish': the reference is
   clarified in *DN*: '153 fish taken in the Sea of Galilee = (12 Apostles)² & (Trinity)²' (703), which Beckett took from Dean Inge's
   chapter on 'Nature Mysticism and Symbolism' in *Christian
   Mysticism*: 'Yet surely there is a vast difference between seeing
   in the "glorious sky embracing all" a type of "our Maker's love",
   and analysing the 153 fish caught in the Sea of Galilee into the
   square of the 12 Apostles & the square of the 3 Persons of the
   Trinity' (272).

'gaff': barbed spear used for fishing.

'closed his eyes . . . vision': in the 1930s Beckett equated writing,
   and the writing of poetry in particular, with sight and vision;
   often this is linked, as here, to Rimbaud's visionary poems, and
   to 'The Drunken Boat' in particular, which Beckett translated
   in May 1932. In a letter to MacGreevy written on 18 October
   1932, Beckett stated that the kind of poetry he wished to write
   would possess something he found 'sometimes in Rimbaud':
   the 'integrity of the eyelids coming down before the brain
   knows of grit in the wind' (*LSB I* 135). Beckett is here also
   referring to what he called Rimbaud's 'eye-suicide – pour des
   visions [for visions]' (letter to MacGreevy, 11 March 1931; *LSB I*
   73), relating to the child in the poem 'Les Poètes de sept ans'
   who rubs his eyes in order to produce distorted visions.

'No, nor anyone else either': echoing Hamlet's 'Man delights not
   me; no, nor woman neither' (II, ii); adapted by Joyce in the
   Scylla and Charybdis episode in *Ulysses*.

'Draff': the title of the last story of *MPTK* as eventually published;
   it was also to be the overall title of the collection until Chatto's
   editor Charles Prentice asked Beckett for a 'livelier title' (25
   September 1933). The word 'draff' is taken from Thomas à
   Kempis's *The Imitation of Christ* (III, xv): 'I saw them delight
   in swine's draff' (*DN* 590). Another possible source is the
   Prologue to Chaucer's *Legend of Good Women*, which also
   furnished Beckett with the title of *Dream*: 'what eyleth thee
   to wryte / The draf of stories, and forgo the corn?' Finally, the
   word also means 'the lees left after brewing'.
'Doyle': the unnamed groundsman in the story 'Draff', left to finish Belacqua's burial.
'zoster': a belt or girdle. Cf. the 'Blaupunkt zoster' in *Dream* (67).
'tumtum': tummy, i.e. stomach.
'Stultum Propter Christum': 'A Fool on Account of Christ', deriving from Thomas à Kempis, *Imitation of Christ* (I, xvii) and
   noted, with translation ('A fool for Xist'), in *DN* (573). Cf. I Corinthians 4:10: 'We are fools for Christ's sake'.
'ikey': slang term for a Jew, especially a Jewish moneylender or
   receiver; but also 'crafty', 'artful'; applied to the pyrotechnist in
   Dream (86).
'doesn't know Bel': Smeraldina's pet-name for Belacqua in
   Dream; Doyle understandably does not know Belacqua, who
   was already dead in 'Draff'. Cf. Hamlet, in conversation with
   Horatio in the graveyard, stating of (the dead) Yorick: 'I knew
   him' (V, i).
'hallowed mould': in Milton, *Paradise Lost* (V, l. 321), Adam is
   'Earth's hallowed mould'.
'like the pile-driver in the story': probably a reference to the
   Brothers Grimm story 'Strong Hans'.
'headstone': at the end of 'Draff', reference is made to 'the company of headstones sighing and gleaming like bones' (*MPTK*
   190). Beckett describes his father's headstone in a letter to
   MacGreevy, 27 July 1933.

'machine-moujik': a moujik is a Russian peasant or serf, here
  potentially undertaking factory work.

'Fool': unto Christ, as Doyle's tattoo indicates.

'I am the body': as in the Eucharist, setting up the parallel
  between Belacqua and Christ in this scene.

'natural body . . . spiritual body': the distinction as made by Paul
  in the Bible: 'It is sown a natural body; it is raised a spiritual
  body. There is a natural body, and there is a spiritual body'
  (I Corinthians 15:44). Beckett cites this passage, and the
  preceding four verses, in a letter to Georges Duthuit of February 1950: 'De ce salaud de Paul j'ai dû te citer un fragment du
  passage suivant' (*LSB II* 180).

'went away and came back': the first of many times Doyle goes
  away to relieve himself.

'Reach hither': echoing Christ's words to the doubter Thomas:
  'Reach hither thy finger, and behold my hands; and reach
  hither thy hand, and thrust it into my side: and be not faithless,
  but believing' (John 20:27).

'a little cavity': in a letter to MacGreevy of 18 October 1932,
  Beckett states that of his poems he prefers those which are not
  'construits' and are 'written above an abscess and not out of a
  cavity' (*LSB I* 134).

'the blue bitch's affront': in 'Walking Out', Belacqua's dog
  urinates over the vagabond's trousers, who responds with a
  voice 'devoid of rancour' (*MPTK* 104). The Beckett family had
  Kerry Blue terriers.

'dunderhead': 'ponderously stupid person' (*OED*); employed by
  Sterne in *Tristram Shandy* (IX, xxv).

'dolt on some Christ's account': a fool, again referring to Doyle's
  tattoo.

'I'll lay you six to four': cf. the bets placed on Hamlet's swords-
  manship.

'pentacle': in the typescript, Beckett had initially written
  'quincunx'.

'bottle not of stout but of schnapps': reference to the fact that in
   'Draff' the groundsman Doyle drinks Guinness (*MPTK* 183).
'flat themes': in 'Draff', these are 'the ancient punctured themes
   recurring, creeping up the treble out of sound' (*MPTK* 183).
'bougie': French for 'wax-candle'.
'amethyst': the word means 'not drunken' or 'not intoxicated',
   deriving from the belief that the stone could prevent intoxica-
   tion; it thus does not give alcohol 'a fair chance'.
'temptation and commercial travelling': from Thomas à Kempis,
   Imitation of Christ (III, 1), as noted in *DN*: 'this frail life that is
   all temptation & knighthood' (596). Cf. also *Dream* 3 and 45.
'my numerous wives and admirers': a reference to the various
   ('fair to middling') women with whom Belacqua has relation-
   ships in *MPTK*.
'privy, papered': taken from Burton (I, 23), and noted in *DN* as
   'putid songsters & their carmina quae legunt cacantes' (727).
   The Latin is from an epigram by Martial, and translates as
   'poems which people read at stool'. Beckett quotes the line in a
   letter to MacGreevy of 8 November 1931 (*LSB I* 94).
'peccadilloes': minor sins or offences.
'chaff': an entry in *DN* (1174) quotes Chaucer: 'Let be the chaf, &
   wryt wel of the corn' (Skeat, A text, l. 529).
'Irish Statesman': the *Irish Statesman* was a journal edited by
   AE (George Russell); first published on 15 September 1923, it
   folded on 12 April 1930. AE turned down two pieces of writing
   Beckett had submitted to the journal, possibly the short story
   'Assumption' in summer 1929 and a poem in spring 1930. AE's
   interest in the psyche is evident from the title of one of his
   articles, 'The Poet and his Psyche'.
'Mr Quin': the reference here is to 'Hairy' Capper Quin, Belacqua's
   best man and, after his death in 'Draff', the man who replaces
   him in the affections of the Smeraldina. Although he is bald,
   his name 'Hairy' suggests potency, and he may be father of
   Smeraldina's babies mentioned in this story. A character named

'Quin' appears in the early drafts of *Watt*, then again in *Mercier and Camier* (as 'someone who does not exist'), *Malone Dies* and the unpublished French story 'Ici personne'.

'to adopt the happy expression of Mr Quin': misremembering the Smeraldina's words in 'Draff': 'Home Hairy' (*MPTK* 183).

'last long home': referring to death, or rather the kind of ultimate annihilation which has so far escaped Belacqua.

'the sty': Beckett had originally written 'most of my week-ends'.

'mot of some note': only of note in that it is an elaborate revision of the following line (as iterated by Hairy Quin in 'Draff').

'stinging . . . Death': citing the Biblical 'O death, where is thy sting?' (I Corinthians 15:55), quoted *verbatim* in 'Draff' (*MPTK* 186).

'mental note': reflecting Beckett's own creative practice of 'notesnatching' from his reading (letter to MacGreevy, early August 1931).

'Limbo': where those who are not saved but did not sin reside; in Dante's *Inferno*, the first circle of hell. Cf. *Dream* (44, 50, 63, 181 and 188) and the poem 'Casket of Pralinen' (*CP* 32).

'nip in the wombbud': anticipating Mr Rooney's question in 'All That Fall': 'Did you ever wish to kill a child? [. . .] Nip some young doom in the bud' (25).

'cyanosis': cf. 'cynasoed [*sic*] face' (*DN* 1020); Beckett's source is Sir William Osler's *The Principles and Practice of Medicine* (1892), designed for the use of practitioners and students of medicine, and specifically the section on 'Alcoholism'. Cyanosis is an effect of excessive alcohol consumption. The word or versions of the word appear in *Dream* (62), the poems 'For Future Reference' and 'Casket of Pralinen' (*CP* 28 and 32), the story 'Love and Lethe' (*MPTK* 92) and *Murphy* (98).

'glump like a fluke in a tup': Irish slang for 'sulk like a worm in a gut'.

'Gonococcus': the bacterium *Neisseria gonorrhoeae*, the cause of gonorrhoea.

'three score years and ten': seventy years, traditionally seen as the span of life, as in Psalm 90:10.

'hot cockles': related to the saying 'to warm the cockles of your
    heart'; in this context a scorning of the seeking for happiness.
'Réchauffé cockles': reheated cockles of the heart, so to speak.
'Communist painter and decorator': who also appears in *Dream*
    (219).
'she spouts, the Mick I know': a further reference to Melville's
    Moby-Dick.
'great greedy wild free human heart': said of Luther in Carlyle's
    On Heroes, Hero-Worship and the Heroic in History (370), as
    noted in *DN*: 'the great greedy wild free human heart of him'
    (281). Cf. *Dream* (196).
'embarrassed caterpillar . . . origins': as the reference to 'origins'
    implies, Beckett alludes to Darwin's *Origin of Species*, which
    he read in summer 1932. In chapter VII on 'Instinct', Darwin
    describes the findings of his colleague Huber, who observed
    that if a caterpillar were interrupted in building its hammock
    and taken to another at an earlier or similar point of comple-
    tion, it would simply finish the work from where it had left
    off; 'if, however, a caterpillar were taken out of a hammock
    made up, for instance, to the third stage, and were put into
    one finished up to the sixth stage, so that much of its work was
    already done for it, far from deriving any benefit from this,
    it was much embarrassed, and in order to complete its ham-
    mock, seemed forced to start from the third stage, where it had
    left off, and thus tried to complete the already finished work'
    (my emphasis). Beckett also uses the anecdote in *Murphy*,
    as Miss Counihan stops in mid-sentence, and will have to go
    back to the beginning 'like Darwin's caterpillar' (130).
'smoke the reference': cf. Fielding, *Tom Jones*, where the expres-
    sion occurs more than once (e.g. IV, 10).
'Monkeybrand': brand of soap. Beckett had originally written
    'Monkeyface' in the typescript.
'ostentatiously eased': the pressure on Doyle's bladder
    increasing.

'clockwork': in *Dream*, Balzac's world is described as being popu-
lated by 'clockwork cabbages' (119) and the character Chas is a
'clockwork fiend' (203). In 'A Wet Night' this is replaced by 'this
clockwork Bartlett' (*MPTK* 50).

'voice': Belacqua becomes a 'voice'; in Ovid's *Metamorphoses*
only the voice and then the bones remain of Echo as she pines
away.

'eyes full of tears': in 'What a Misfortune', Belacqua's eyes are
'moist' after Hairy Quin told him that 'You perish in your own
plenty' (*MPTK*), the quotation deriving from Augustine (III, xii)
and entered in *DN*: 'The son of these tears shall not perish' (89).
This in turn is connected with the 'babies' in Zaborovna's eyes.

'mewl': whimper of an infant child.

'buckled discourse': in a letter of early September 1931 Beckett
told MacGreevy that 'one has to buckle the wheel of one's poem
somehow or run the risk of Nordau's tolerance' (*LSB I* 87).
Beckett had recently read Max Nordau's book *Degeneration*
(1892).

'honour your father . . . Göthe': cf. Renard, *Journal* (22 February
1890), 'Honore ton père, et ta mère, et Virgile', underlined in
Beckett's personal copy and entered into *DN* (214). It appears
in *Dream* (178) with Goethe substituted for Virgil, as here.

'Bright . . . wind': quoting line 7 of Tennyson's poem 'The Poet's
Mind', of which several lines are quoted in *DN* (1159) and
Dream (87).

'Keyed up': 'to regulate the pitch of the strings of a musical instrument' (*OED*). Frequently, as here, used figuratively to raise up
or stimulate feelings or thoughts. Here Belacqua is in such a
state of excitement that he (or his strings) threatens to 'snap'.

'error, or, better, blunder': adapting a line copied into *DN* (37),
'Worse than a crime, a blunder', taken from Lockhart (255),
who is in turn quoting Fouché on the execution of the Duke
d'Enghien in 1804. The phrase 'Butter was a blunder' appears
in 'Dante and the Lobster' (*MPTK* 12).

'throat olive convulsed': i.e. the Adam's apple; the word 'throat-olive' is in *DN* (526), quoting Giles, *The Civilisation of China* (131).

'bumped off': as Belacqua was in the story 'Yellow'.

'Horror! It was dawning': like Hamlet's ghost, Belacqua must depart before it dawns.

'Dawn, aborting': as the cow did earlier.

'layette': 'A complete outfit of garments, toilet articles, and bedding for a new-born child' (*OED*).

'Pfui': German for 'yuck'.

'bist Du nicht willig': German for 'if you are not willing'; quoting Goethe's poem 'Erlkönig' – the line in the original continues 'then I'll use force'.

'Bating': meaning 'except', the word also appears in 'Dante and Lobster' and 'What a Misfortune' (*MPTK* 17 and 139).

'inaudible': having asked Zaborovna to 'speak up', Belacqua now cannot hear what Doyle is saying; as above based on Virgil in Dante's *Inferno*, who is 'chi per lungo silenzio parea fioco (hoarse from long silence)' (TCD MS10966/1, 1r).

'de rigueur': French, required by custom or fashion.

'crazy old chronology': a common complaint in Beckett's early writing; cf. the criticism of the 'lovely Pythagorean chain-chant solo of cause and effect' in *Dream* (10).

'begin with the Dove and end up with the Son': a reference to the Annunciation where the Holy Spirit appears to the Virgin Mary as a dove.

'passes my persimmon': i.e. 'passes my comprehension', citing Thomas de Quincey's 'On Murder Considered as One of the Fine Arts', as noted in *DN*: 'It passes my persimmon to say . . .' (718). Also used in *Dream* (49).

'keep your bake shut': Dublin slang for 'keep your mouth shut'; the phrase is in *DN* (641) and used in *Dream* (115).

'Game ball . . . again': i.e. game over; 'again' as the phrase has been used by the vagabond in 'Walking Out' (*MPTK* 104), where it prematurely ends a conversation.

'pastoral days': referring to the story 'Walking Out', which
describes Belacqua's trip to the Dublin mountains.

'Thanatos': Greek for death.

'reintegrate the matrix': an entry in *DN*, taken from Gaultier's
De Kant à Nietzsche (6), reads: 'Monotheistic fiction bicuspid:
Bible & Plato: torn by the forceps of Sophism from the violated
matrix of Pure Reason . . . !' (1149).

'death came and undid me': cf. T. S. Eliot's *The Waste Land*:
'A crowd flowed over London Bridge, so many, / I had not
thought death had undone so many' (ll. 62–3); itself, as Eliot's
note indicates, from Dante's *Inferno*: 'And behind it came so
long a train of people, that I should never have believed death
had undone so many' (III, 55–7).

'velleities': wish or inclination without action or effort. T. S. Eliot
uses the word in the poem 'Portrait of a Lady'. Also found in
Dream (43 and 152).

'gull . . . Gael': possibly playing on Gall and Gael, foreigner in or
native of Ireland.

'did after all reach forth': reprising the story of the doubter
Thomas.

'they all do': with a possible nod toward the title of Mozart's
opera *Così fan tutte*. Also in *Dream* (223) and 'A Wet Night'
(*MPTK* 69).

'dust of a dove's heart': noted in *DN* (865) and taken from Burton
(III, 132). Applied in *Dream* to the Smeraldina (31) and the Alba
(111).

'Nichol's box': the firm of undertakers responsible for the burial
of Beckett's father, William Beckett, was called Nichols and Co.

'saturnine': used here both in the sense of 'gloomy' and as relating to lead.

'agitato': Latin for 'agitated', used in music as a dynamic marking.

'Gottlob': German for 'Thank heavens'.

'knock-about': the word appears, without hyphen, in Beckett's
1934 review of Sean O'Casey's *Windfalls* (*Dis* 82).

'show a glim': cf. Dickens, *Oliver Twist*: 'Show a glim, Toby.'

'Adam that good old man . . . service': quoting Orlando's words to
   Adam in Shakespeare's *As You Like It* (II, iii) – 'O good old man'
   – whom he also praises for his 'constant service.'

'Light and sweetness': cited in a letter to Nuala Costello of 27
   February 1934 (with 'obliterate gloom' rather than as here
   'obliterate dole'); possibly from Matthew Arnold, *Culture
   and Anarchy* (1869), according to which the aim of culture
   is 'to make all men live in an atmosphere of sweetness and
   light.'

'consume like a spider away': entered in *DN* as 'to consume away
   like a spider (soul)' (135), and taken from Augustine (VII, x). Cf.
   Dream (68, 73).

'greasing the palm of some saint': Beckett is possibly referring
   to the practice of having to pay to see paintings in churches; a
   version of votive candles.

'Give it a name': colloquial for 'what would you like to drink', also
   used in *Dream* (203) and 'A Wet Night' (*MPTK* 51).

'link-boy': in the days before street lighting, boys who would
   carry flaming torches to light the way for pedestrians.

'anxiomaniac': the word 'anxiomania', meaning 'frenzied
   anguish', is noted in *DN* (659), taken from Nordau's *Degeneration* (226).

'flaws of tramontane': adapting a note in *DN*, 'flaws of wind (Little Dorrit)' (1036), from ch. 9 of Dickens's novel. 'Tramontane'
   is the Italian for a north wind. Cf. *Dream* (139) and 'Yellow'
   (*MPTK* 163).

'cabal of vipers': a reference to François Mauriac's novel *Le Nœud
   de vipères* (*The Knot of Vipers*, 1932).

'Mark Disney': thinking of Walt Disney?

'Goldwasser': a liqueur produced in Danzig; in *Dream*, the barmaid Eva prefers Goldwasser to Steinhäger (99).

'buttoned up': Beckett is referring here to Beethoven, both in
   terms of the letter in which the composer 'unbuttoned' him-

self, as well as the so-called 'unbuttoned' Seventh Symphony. *DN* contains the entry 'the 7th & 8th aufgeknoepft' (1107), taken from Romain Rolland's *Vie de Beethoven*. Cf. *Dream* (138, 188 and 227) and 'What a Misfortune' (*MPTK* 140).

'to bite it off': with a nod towards an entry in *DN* (819), adapted from Burton (II, 186): 'The beaver bites off his balls – that he may live'. It reappears in *Dream* as 'a very persuasive chapter of Natural History' (63), and in *Murphy* (129).

'handful of stones': in Ovid's *Metamorphoses*, Echo, scorned by Narcissus, wastes away until only her voice and her bones, changed to stones, remain.

'snuff of candle': quoting Burton (II, 151), as evidenced by a note in *DN*: 'his memory stinks like the snuff of a candle' (816). Cf. *Dream* (120).

'So it goes in the world': the story ends with a repetition of one of Beckett's favourite sentiments taken from the Brothers Grimm story 'How the Cat and the Mouse Set Up House'.

LETTERS FROM CHARLES PRENTICE
AT CHATTO & WINDUS
TO SAMUEL BECKETT

Charles Prentice to Samuel Beckett, 25 SEPTEMBER 1933
[UoR MS 2444/Letter Book 150/134-5]

Dear Sam,

Chatto's would be delighted to publish the stories, and we would like to make you the following offer. Short stories are chancey things, on which the library and the bookseller turn a poached-egg eye. So it is a little difficult to suggest an advance, especially as 'Proust' has earned only two-thirds of his, but I hope that £25 will seem to you fair. [. . .]

The book is just long enough to sell at 7/6d., and we'd publish early next year. [. . .]

Can you think of a livelier title? I don't suppose many people know what 'Draff' is, but if they look it up, they will be put off.

[. . .]

Hurray too if you manage that extra story. [. . .]

Yours ever,

Charles

Charles Prentice to Samuel Beckett, 29 SEPTEMBER 1933
[UoR MS 2444/Letter Book 150/196–7]

Dear Sam,

[...]

Many thanks for giving so amiable a think to the title of the book. We also prefer 'More Pricks than Kicks'. It's much better than 'Draff', I am sure, but if you light on another, the substitution can easily be made. [...]

Another 10,000 words, or even 5,000 for that matter, would, I am certain, help the book, and it would be lovely if you manage to reel them out. It would be necessary to have the complete MS. before sending it to the printers, in order that they could plan accurately the requisite number of pages. But we could easily wait a month or six weeks before sending the MS. off, and doubtless you'll know by then whether an addition is possible or not.

Yours ever,

Charles

Charles Prentice to Samuel Beckett, 4 OCTOBER 1933
[UoR MS 2444/Letter Book 150/245]

My dear Sam,

[...]

I'm delighted that Belacqua Lazarus will be walking again shortly. Let me shake him by the hand as soon as you can buy a ticket for him. Will his next appearance be a prick or a kick? The more I think of it, the more I like that title. [...]

Yours ever,

Charles

Charles Prentice to Samuel Beckett, 2 NOVEMBER 1933
[UoR MS 2444/Letter Book 151/138]

Dear Sam,

[. . .]

'Echo's Bones' is a tasty title, and, from the tone of your postcard, I infer that the 10,000 yelps will soon be parcelled up and on their way to Holyhead. Good for Belacqua. Give him up? What next! [. . .]

Yours ever,

Charles

Charles Prentice to Samuel Beckett, 10 NOVEMBER 1933
[UoR MS 2444/Letter Book 151/241]

My dear Sam,

What a big one! Ever so many thanks for 'Echo's Bones'. I shall read it with delight over this week-end. [. . .]

Yours ever,

Charles

Charles Prentice to Samuel Beckett, 13 NOVEMBER 1933
[UoR MS 2444/Letter Book 151/277]

Dear Sam,

It is a nightmare. Just too terribly persuasive. It gives me the jim-jams. The same horrible and immediate switches of the focus, and the same wild unfathomable energy of the population. There are chunks I don't connect with. I am so sorry to feel like this. Perhaps it is only over the details, and I may have a correct inkling of the main impression. I am sorry, for I hate to be dense, but I hope I am not altogether insensitive. 'Echo's Bones' certainly did land on me with a wallop.

Do you mind if we leave it out of the book – that is, publish 'More Pricks than Kicks' in the original form in which you sent it in? Though it's on the short side, we'll still be able to price it at 7/6d. 'Echo's Bones' would, I am sure, lose the book a great many readers. People will shudder and be puzzled and confused; and they won't be keen on analysing the shudder. I am certain that 'Echo's Bones' would depress the sales very considerably.

I hate having to say this, as well as falling behind scratch myself, and I hope you will forgive as far as you can. Please try to make allowances for us; the future of the book affects you as well.

This is a dreadful débâcle – on my part, not on yours, God save the mark. But I have to own up to it. A failure, a blind-spot, call it what I may. Yet the only plea for mercy I can make is that the icy touch of those revenant fingers was too much for me. I am sitting on the ground, and ashes are on my head.

Please write kindly,

Yours ever,

[Charles]

Charles Prentice to Samuel Beckett, 17 NOVEMBER 1933
[UoR MS 2444/Letter Book 151/325]

Dear Sam,

Your forgiveness is like oil of absolution – but I cannot absolve myself for my failure. Thank you very, very much. If I may, I'd like to keep 'Echo's Bones' a little longer, but we'll go ahead with the setting up of the book. [. . .]

Ever yours,

Charles

Charles Prentice to Samuel Beckett, 4 DECEMBER 1933
[UoR MS 2444/Letter Book 152/82]

Dear Sam,

I return 'Echo's Bones'. To the boneyard with me! Proofs are streaming in, and you will have had a good lot by now. I hope you like the look of the page etc. [. . .]

Yours ever,

Charles

Charles Prentice to Samuel Beckett, 11 DECEMBER 1933
[UoR MS 2444/Letter Book 152/176]

Dear Sam,

Many thanks for the duplicates of the remainder of Belacqua's proofs. I am glad you have put in that new little bit at the end. It is a decided improvement. Thank you too for the secret song of the groundsman – zoological vistas of a truly classico-romantic kind! I am proud to be a participator in his confidence. [. . .]

Ever,

Charles

BIBLIOGRAPHY

Works Cited

SAMUEL BECKETT – ARCHIVAL MATERIAL

'Echo's Bones', typescript, Baker Library, Dartmouth College.

'Echo's Bones', typescript, A. J. Leventhal Collection, Harry Ransom Humanities Research Center, University of Texas at Austin.

'German Diaries' (6 notebooks), Beckett International Foundation, University of Reading.

'Ici personne ne vient jamais', unpublished prose text, typescript, Beckett International Foundation, University of Reading, MS1656/4.

Letters to Barbara Bray, Trinity College Library, Dublin, MS10948/1.

Letters to Ruby Cohn, Beckett International Foundation, University of Reading, MS5100.

Letters to Jocelyn Herbert, Beckett International Foundation, University of Reading, MS5200.

Letters to Thomas MacGreevy, Trinity College Library Dublin, MS10402.

Notes from Samuel Beckett's lectures at Trinity College Dublin, taken by Rachel Dobbin (Burrows), Trinity College Library Dublin, MIC60.

Notes on Dante's *The Divine Comedy*, Beckett International Foundation, University of Reading, MS4123.

Notes on Dante, Trinity College Library Dublin, MS10966/1.

Notes on Philosophy, Trinity College Library Dublin, MS10967.

Notes on Psychology, Trinity College Library Dublin, MS10971/8.

Notes on the 'Trueborn Jackeen' and 'Cow', Trinity College Library Dublin, MS10971/2.

Transcription of Giacomo Leopardi's poem 'A Se Stesso', Trinity College Library Dublin, 10971/9.

'Whoroscope' Notebook, Beckett International Foundation, University of Reading, MS3000.

SAMUEL BECKETT – PUBLICATIONS

'A Piece of Monologue' and 'All That Fall', in *The Collected Shorter Plays* (New York: Grove Press, 2010).

Collected Poems of Samuel Beckett, ed. Seán Lawlor and John Pilling (New York: Grove Press, 2014).

'Company', 'Ill Seen, Ill Said', and 'Worstward Ho', in *Nohow On* (New York: Grove Press, 1995).

Dream of Fair to Middling Women (Dublin: Black Cat Press, 1992).

Disjecta: Miscellaneous Writings and a Dramatic Fragment, ed. Ruby Cohn (New York: Grove Press, 1995).

Endgame and Act Without Words (New York: Grove Press, 2009).

'The Expelled', 'The Calmative', and 'The End', in *Stories and Texts for Nothing* (New York: Grove Press, 1994).

'First Love', 'Fizzles', and 'Stirrings Still', in *The Complete Short Prose 1929–1989*, ed. S. E. Gontarski (New York: Grove Press, 1997).

Krapp's Last Tape and Other Dramatic Pieces (New York: Grove Press, 2009).

The Letters of Samuel Beckett, vol. 1: 1929–1940, ed. Martha Dow Fehsenfeld, Lois More Overbeck, George Craig, and Dan Gunn (Cambridge: Cambridge University Press, 2011).

The Letters of Samuel Beckett, vol. 2: 1941–1956, ed. George Craig, Martha Dow Fehsenfeld, Dan Gunn, and Lois More Overbeck (Cambridge: Cambridge University Press, 2011).

Mercier and Camier (New York: Grove Press, 2011).

More Pricks than Kicks (New York: Grove Press, 1995).

Murphy (New York: Grove Press, 2011).

'Proust' in *The Poems, Short Fiction, and Criticism of Samuel Beckett* (New York: Grove Press, 2007).

Three Novels: Molloy, Malone Dies, The Unnamable (New York: Grove Press, 2009).

Waiting for Godot (New York: Grove Press, 2011).

Watt (New York: Grove Press, 2009).

OTHER WRITERS

Alfieri, Vittorio, *The Autobiography of Vittorio Alfieri, Tragic Poet*, ed. and trans. C. Edwards Lester (New York: Paine and Burgess, 1845).

Augustine, St, *Confessions*, trans. E. B. Pusey (London: Everyman's Library, 1907) (chapter divisions however cited from Henry Chadwick's edition, Oxford University Press, 1991).

Bourrienne, Louis Antoine Fauvelet de, *Memoirs of Napoleon* (London: Richard Bentley, 1836).

Bouvier, J. B., *Dissertatio in Sextum Decalogi Praeceptum, et Supplementum ad Tractatum de Matrimonio* (Paris: Facultatis Theologiae Bibliopolas, 1852).

Burton, Robert, *The Anatomy of Melancholy*, 3 vols, ed. Holbrook Jackson (London: Dent [Everyman's Library], 1932).

Carlyle, Thomas, *On Heroes, Hero-Worship and the Heroic in History* (London: J. M. Dent, 1908).

Chaucer, Geoffrey, *The Student's Chaucer, being a Complete Edition of his Works*, ed. W. W. Skeat (London and New York: Macmillan & Co., 1894).

Cooper, William M. [James Glass Bertram], *Flagellation and the Flagellants* (London: Chatto and Windus, 1887).

Dante, *The Divine Comedy*, 'Temple Classics' (London: J. M. Dent, 1900–1 (*Inferno* 1900; *Purgatorio* 1901; *Paradiso* 1901)).

Garnier, Pierre, *Onanisme seul et à deux sous toutes ses formes et leurs consequences*, 10th edn (Paris: Libraire Garnier Frères, n.d. [c.1895]).

Gaultier, Jules de, *De Kant à Nietzsche*, 10th edn (Paris: Mercure de France, 1930).

Giles, H. A., *The Civilisation of China* (London: Williams and Norgate, n.d. [1911]).

Homer, *L'Odyssée*, trans. Victor Bérard, 3 vols (Paris: Société d'édition 'Les Belles Lettres', 1925).

Inge, W. R., *Christian Mysticism* (London: Methuen, 1899).

Jeans, James, *The Universe Around Us* (Cambridge: University Press, 1929).

Kempis, Thomas à, *The Imitation of Christ*, trans. John K. Ingram (London: Kegan Paul, Trench, Turner & Co., 1893).

Legouis, Émile, and Louis Cazamian, *Histoire de la littérature anglaise* (Paris: Hachette, 1929).

Lockhart, J. G., *The History of Napoleon Bonaparte* (London: William Tegg, n.d. (1867?)).

Mahaffy, J. P., *Descartes* (Edinburgh: Blackwood, 1880).

Nordau, Max, *Degeneration* (London: William Heinemann, 1895).

Osler, William, *The Principles and Practice of Medicine* (New York: D. Appleton & Co., 1892).

Praz, Mario, *The Romantic Agony*, trans. Angus Davidson, 2nd edn (London: Oxford University Press, 1954).

Renard, Jules, *Le Journal de Jules Renard 1887–1910*, 4 vols (Paris: François Bernouard, 1927).

Ruskin, John, *Modern Painters* (Sunnyside, Orpington and London: G. Allen, 1888).

Taylor, Jeremy, *The Rule and Exercises of Holy Living and Holy Dying* (London: Longmans, Green & Co., 1926).

Toynbee, Paget, *Dictionary of Proper Names and Notable Matters in the Works of Dante* (Oxford: Clarendon Press, 1898).

Ueberweg, Friedrich, *A History of Philosophy, from Thales to the Present Time*, vol. 1: *History of Ancient and Medieval Philosophy*, trans. George S. Morris (London: Hodder and Stoughton, 1872).

Critical Studies of Samuel Beckett

Ackerley, Chris, 'Samuel Beckett and the Bible: A Guide', *Journal of Beckett Studies* 9.1 (Autumn 1999), 53–126.

——, *'Demented Particulars': The Annotated Murphy* (Edinburgh: Edinburgh University Press, 2010).

——, *Obscure Locks, Simple Keys: The Annotated Watt* (Edinburgh: Edinburgh University Press, 2010).

Ackerley, Chris and S. E. Gontarski, *The Faber Companion to Samuel Beckett* (London: Faber and Faber, 2006).

Admussen, Richard, *The Samuel Beckett Manuscripts: A Study* (Boston: G. K. Hall, 1979).

Atik, Anne, *How It Was: A Memoir of Samuel Beckett* (London: Faber and Faber, 2001).

Campbell, Julie, '"Echo's Bones" and Beckett's Disembodied Voices', in *Samuel Beckett Today / Aujourd'hui* 11: *Samuel Beckett: Endlessness in the Year 2000/Fin sans Fin en l'an 2000*, ed. Angela Moorjani and Carola Veit (Amsterdam: Rodopi, 2001), 454–60.

Fernández, José Francisco, '"Echo's Bones": Samuel Beckett's Lost Story of Afterlife', *Journal of the Short Story in English* 52 (Spring 2009), 115–24.

Hunkeler, Thomas, *Echos de l'ego dans l'oeuvre de Samuel Beckett* (Paris: L'Harmattan, 1997).

Lawlor, Seán, 'Making a Noise to Drown an Echo: Allusion and Quotation in the Early Poems of Samuel Beckett', unpublished PhD thesis, University of Reading, 2008.

——, '"O Death Where Is Thy Sting?" Finding Words for the Big Ideas', in *Beckett and Death*, ed. Steven Barfield, Matthew Feldman and Philip Tew (London: Continuum, 2009), 50–71.

McNaughton, James: 'Samuel Beckett's "Echo's Bones": Politics and Entailment in the Irish Free State', *Modern Fiction Studies* (forthcoming).

Nixon, Mark, '"Belacqua redivivus": Beckett's short story "Echo's Bones"', *Limit(e) Beckett* 1 (2010).

Pilling, John, *Beckett before Godot* (Cambridge: Cambridge University Press, 1997).

——, *A Companion to Dream of Fair to Middling Women* (Tallahassee, FL: Journal of Beckett Studies Books, 2004).

——, 'The Uses of Enchantment: Beckett and the Fairy Tale', *Samuel Beckett Today / Aujourd'hui* 21 (2009), 75–85.

——, *Samuel Beckett's More Pricks Than Kicks* (London: Continuum, 2011).

Rabinovitz, Rubin, *The Development of Samuel Beckett's Fiction* (Chicago: University of Illinois Press, 1984).

Tajiri, Yoshiki, *Samuel Beckett and the Prosthetic Body: The Organs and Senses in Modernism* (Basingstoke: Palgrave Macmillan, 2006).

Van Hulle, Dirk: 'Figures of Script: The Development of Beckett's Short Prose and the "Aesthetic of Inaudibilities"', in *A Companion to Samuel Beckett,* ed. S. E. Gontarski (Chichester: Wiley-Blackwell, 2010), 244–62.

——, and Mark Nixon: *Samuel Beckett's Library* (Cambridge: Cambridge University Press, 2013).